Event Field

by Elaine Morrison

Event Field

This is a work of fiction. All of the characters, names, incidents,
organizations, and dialogue in this novel are either the products
of the author's imagination or are used fictitiously.

iUniverse books may be ordered through booksellers or by contacting:

iUniverse
1663 Liberty Drive
Bloomington, IN 47403
www.iuniverse.com
1-800-Authors (1-800-288-4677)

ISBN: 978-0-595-53155-4 (pbk)
ISBN: 978-0-595-63217-6 (ebk)

Library of Congress Control Number: 2009927159

Printed in the United States of America

iUniverse rev. date: 4/27/2009

Zmam
copyright 2005 by Elaine Morrison
first printing 2005 Kamloops, Canada
Library & Archives Canada Cataloguing in Publication
Morrison, Elaine, 1968-
Zmam / by Elaine Morrison.
ISBN 978-0-9739682-0-6
I. Title.
PS8626.O758Z44 2005   C813'.6   C2005-906934-1

The Draft
copyright 2006 by Elaine Morrison
first printing 2006 Kamloops, Canada
The Draft / by Elaine Morrison.
ISBN 978-0-9739682-2-2
I. Title.
PS8626.O758D73 2006   C813'.6   C2006-903406-0
Comprises book 2 of a fictional series
and follows in the Zmam drama.

Counterpoint
copyright 2008 by Elaine Morrison
first printing 2008 Toronto, Canada
Counterpoint / by Elaine Morrison
ISBN 978-0-973982-5-5
I. Title
PS8626.O758C68 2008   C813'.6   C2008-903820-7
Counterpoint comprises book 3 of a fictional series
following Zmam and The Draft.

evil **purpose**; false testimony; muzzle   זְמָם, ז'

‖

planning; intelligence; craftinɛss; sagacity   מְזִמָּה, נ', ר', ־מוֹת

the Divine   ה' -

זָמַם

his nose, his anger   אַפּוֹ

to flow, d i s t i l   נָזַל, פ״ע

βy the mouth; at the opening, in the orifice   בַּפֶּה

‖

87

‖

fine gold   פָּז, ז'

‖

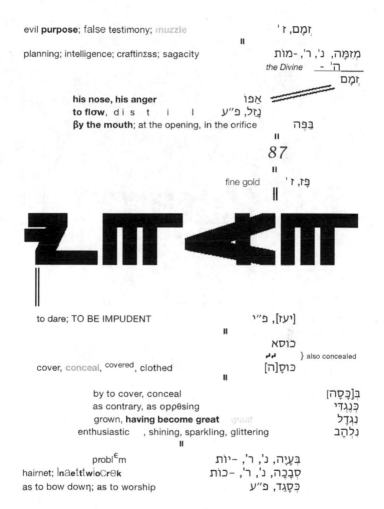

to dare; TO BE IMPUDENT   [יעז], פ״י

‖

כוסא

} also concealed

cover, conceal, covered, clothed   כּוּסָ[ה]

‖

by to cover, conceal   בְּ[כָסָה]

as contrary, as oppθsing   כְּנֶגְדִי

grown, **having become great**   נִגְדָּל

enthusiastic , shining, sparkling, glittering   נִלְהָב

‖

problɛm   בְּעָיָה, נ', ר', ־יוֹת

hairnet; lnaettlwioCrɐk   סְבָכָה, נ', ר', ־כוֹת

as to bow dowη; as to worship   כְּסָגַד, פ״ע

Zmam

book 1

<u>Chapter One</u>

Down the road exiting Jerusalem toward Jordan, called a highway but it was one easterly lane and another three-quarter gravelly falling over the hill joke rudely dropping into sand and rock to disappear all traces. Down winding past Hebrew University perched atop Mount Scopus the barrier, accelerating with the current in its descent from Israel to the Occupied Territories. Down curving through the baked army checkpoint, gripping cliffside as Maaleh Adomim's floating orange-capped villas witness the plummeting way to the Dead Sea, rounding to lose reference of the sentinel broadcast tower to the desert. Gadi traced his foot behind the brake to identify the existence of an obstruction, then repeated the exercise to pluck up the accelerator. This wasn't going to be the solution so he held tight the wheel and proceeded along his imaginary list. Release while applying emergency brake. No, that would not be effective at his speed.

It was the sight of her husband steering with one hand as hunched over he strained with the other for the handle by his feet and the concentrated stare that accompanied ensuing awkward gingerly foot-pressing with his knee in his face that wordlessly caught Tal's dread even more than his lunatic driving.

The transmission wouldn't allow Gadi into lower gear. He tried turning the key to extinguish the ignition, but it was locked. So he veered off the edge of the road positioning the car's wheels in the ditch to reduce speed. And as the ditch sheered away Gadi rejoined the lane proper only then to cross centre line and screech the entire driver's side of the metal cage against layered cut rock.

Oncoming traffic. Gadi threw their crumpled white box over the red Judean Hills. Vast expanses of wild heat swallowed up their tiny insignificant existence. In a haze the occupants dragged each other out and distanced themselves from the wreck before collapsing into the dirt to watch it explode.

As the heap burnt away in the sun the vehicle which had confronted them back on the road and unwittingly effected their plunge was turning around.

Gadi and Tal glimpsed their rescuers in disjointed fragments spanning the duration of the haphazard covering of their wounds, endless tense bantering in Hebrew regarding the team's plan of action, the callous clutching of their limbs in transit across the rough terrain and in their brutal ascent to somewhere close to civilization. They all packed inside the rescuers' much too small transport and tore on their way. Then nothing.

The media reporting the demise of the family cited Gadi and Tal as physicist dissidents who for the past few years had been advocating improved conditions for the nuclear scientists at the Dimona facility and consequently brought the plant unwanted worldwide attention. Yuli soaked the words from the television and newspapers. They mirrored her sister Tal's paranoia in late night conversations. Incoming calls hit the machine. She closed the shutters and feigned absence. Then finally when everyone was convinced she had really lost her mind Yuli left her apartment and transferred a bulky wad of bills to the hand of her newly hired private investigator.

She worked as a clinical psychologist and her boyfriend had had enough but months of surrendering her paycheque to this clandestine confidant each time in an inspired concocted manner was offering results. Yuli ate the melted cheese toastie she had purchased at a deli blocks away on an abandoned pier in the centre of Tel Aviv's waterfront. Then she unraveled the wrapper and devoured its contents:

Good news. Police files don't mention
bodies at accident scene. No reports of

patients in hospitals or morgues matching descriptions. Car exploded. Need to quietly test car and scene for DNA and bone fragments. Car exploded. Evidence of tampering destroyed if flammable.

"Who's crazy now?" And with every word of the message memorized it was crumpled up like lunch trash and tossed into the Mediterranean. Not to proliferate littering, this was an exception. Her paid sleuth adamantly conveyed the ultra-secrecy of their acquaintance if they were to combat the possible forces behind this even to the point of her never addressing him by name which she couldn't if she wanted to. No name. No office. No paper. No number. No pattern. No trail. Drinking canned mango, walking near carefree people on the beach.

Mystery guy could have been duping her, Yuli understood that much. But it was that first meeting when she looked behind those emerald eyes that had seen far too much for her comfort level that told her he was part man part rat, exactly the person up to the task. His body language would have you opting for the other side of the street should you cross his tracks, an unlikely coupling which kept her uneasy.

Thugs ransacked Gadi and Tal's last estimated position. Operating with frantic efficiency at a site having been left for the most part intact since it was in the middle of nowhere at the bottom of a chasm, the bums combed through the charred mass examining its remains, snapping micro-photos, sawing off steel fragments and bagging the samples. Hopping in a jeep the pair was gone. They bumped along out of sight of the highway and visually scoured their field. "There, five o'clock." A herd of goats.

"And where there are goats there's..."

"A shepherd," the driver muttered.

"And where there's a shepherd there's..."

"A Bedouin camp." This took longer to come into view.

"Meaning?"

"Don't be surprised if they have more trinkets from the crash than we do," he advised as they disembarked.

Re-embarking, "Useless."

"You think?" cranking the engine.

"Tight-lipped."

"Very." His inflection underlined by sudden acceleration was curious.

"Too much?"

"Maybe. No information is also information,

"depending on how it is withheld. By the way, if we're found out and someone gets to you I'm providing a routine survey for an insurance company. You know nothing else."

"I really don't." Laboratory did know, however, a vast number of means by which a perpetrator might undetectably affect an automobile's performance or its passengers. The premise is simple, that the device be temporary. Light paper or plastic blocking the hot exhaust pipe would poison the occupants with carbon monoxide gas and later burn off, ventilation also removing the toxin from the cab. Then there is the class of heavier plastic, material, or rope which may obstruct the workings of brake cords or other critical devices and require fire or preferably an explosion to completely erase, this obviously providing a good indication as to what happens to the people inside. He also knew miles of tracks digging through ditches, traversing the highway to rub against rock sides, and skidding the wheels perpendicular to the direction of travel were the cries of the truth trying to tell of a final struggle.

The cobblestone Promenade in Talpiot watched suns set each night on Jerusalem's old city in reds and gold of incongruous calm. All places have their own feel and sound of the air. Although one may walk on a hill in the centre of town, after the bus has thundered by you are alone in the warmth of the dryness of the breeze silently scanning lower landscapes. And there it is, the unmistakable sense of the Middle East. And there in the thick of it is Yuli. She distanced herself from the faint chatter of china cups and plates by the patrons of the panoramic restaurant, toward and beyond an Arab vendor selling freshly baked bagels accompanied by that little precious packet of olive-tinted zatar spice, out of the visuals of silhouetted young Israeli couples, over the ridge's far side. A gentle sloped modern grassy park. A mosaic path. An ancient well, the end of a historic waterway rising from the south, and reaching deep to her shoulder she unstuck her egg-sized prize from within. Imprisoned in wads of tape was a miniature cassette player begging her ear which was conflictingly eager and wary:

> Progressing smoothly. There is
> conclusively no DNA in the crash area
> so no one died in the car explosion,
> concurring with police paperwork.
> Therefore the bodies must be living or
> deceased somewhere else but oddly

there is no record of that in the expected places.

The trail to the crash fingers the driver fighting a serious vehicular malfunction perhaps disenabling it from stopping. Post-explosion there no longer exists evidence of foul play but that does not eliminate the possibility of the presence of an impediment that burnt away.

I got the impression I was interviewing a witness to the events, but nothing concrete. My intuition says thus there was something to see and a reason not to speak. Terrorism? There would have been declarations, demands, again corpses. Frankly I find the smoothness of this whole abduction highly significant. Life is messy and there are plenty of facts and onlookers to attest to every detail of its occurrences, especially a loud violent motorized rupture and vaporizing adults, unless someone walks behind you sweeping them up. Plausible explanations only account for part of the happenings.

When combining the mechanical failure
and the parties' absence, my
assumption at this point in keeping
with the subjects' professional and
political activities and not discounting
their own subjective fears is that they
have in fact been disappeared and that
this has been ordered and executed
extremely precisely from the highest
levels. Now I know who to look for.

Rewind, eject, and barbecue.

She depressed the first button and with that blades
appeared surgically slicing the rewinding reel as a
syringe squirted upon it a liquid substance. The eject
command fractured its case so exposure to
atmospheric oxygen ignited the butchered contents
while everything burst forth from the deck. By the
time the ill-fated flaming cassette tape parachuted to
earth it was no more. Still startled by the drama of her
shooting incendiary device slash Walkman which she
tucked into her purse for unknown later use, it did
provide a measure of albeit aggressive comedic relief.

"Where are you?" Dreaming of being swallowed by massive waves storming onto boulders dividing land and sea. Scrambling not to lose her footing as they sweep farther inland than expected. She is afraid to drown. Her favourite song plays.

"Do you know that car accidents kill more Israelis than terrorism?" This was commentary in typical style at mealtime, the fare not being half bad. It was in many respects a throwback to army days, minus the jailer. Last week he taunted them with quips of farm country and UFO's, spawning days of debate whether it was just acerbic ribbing or pessimistic conditioning so they would resign themselves to being forgotten. For the moment incarceration wasn't as torturous as one might imagine only since they were still recouping from their injuries and were not fit enough to mentally digest the severity of their predicament, let alone physically protest it. As they would become healthy and whole, however, being cast as prisoners would render itself increasingly more unbearable.

Chapter Two

And what should Aram twist his head to read centred on the blackboard while shuffling in late and parking his supplies but:

administrative detention

the subject before the raucous 150 students in this classroom at the Faculty of Law. And alongside that was a wandering line designating the chunk of board sacrificed to solar glare and therefore off limits for writing. The professor clapped the podium with her hand and waited for the clamor to dissipate.

"So, have we been kidnapped or by some perversion is this legitimate?"

Gadi's eyes pierced Tal and he ran his leathery hand through her hair. "Which answer would you like it to be?"

"...a remnant of English mandatorial law," continued the lecture, "administrative law is still the legal system governing the Occupied Territories. Israeli law generally stops at the Green Line. For example, seat belt regulations do not apply in Yehuda "and Shomron..." The girl beside Aram scribbling furiously leans into his page, pointing, picking up parts she missed. A few seats along the bench-table Americans translate phrases to English. Someone else spills his coffee. "...but Israeli rule of law is extended to its citizens living across the boundary." Noise levels increase as focus wanes and students discuss their views with neighbours at either elbow. Outvoiced, the professor ceases speaking to resume banging the wood for attention. She is extremely patient for this is the norm.

"Then we have rights. There must be arrest warrants, charges we can dispute. Legal proceedings," and from her own declarations Tal derived shades of hope. Until she looked to Gadi who in his worldliness adoringly pitied her.

"...Under administrative detention authorities are not obliged to immediately provide legal counsel nor appearance before a judge for a period of weeks, even months. They are not even required to allow the detainee one phone call to the outside world. Yes," the professor indicated to an agitated student wanting to comment.

"This denial of rights means that to the rest of

"society these people have literally vanished. How are their families supposed to know they're even alive or weren't killed by terrorists or died in a fiery car crash on civilization's periphery?!"

"Exactly. Your name?"

"Aram."

"Something, Gadi. Rules, regulations that have to be followed. Proof. A system we fit into."

"...at the discretion of the authority..."

Gadi held his wife firmly, not in an oppressive manner, but in genuine concern for the reaction she may give to what he was about to say next. "Do you know, Tal, where we fit in the system?" He supported her more, sensing her true despondence in the weight sinking into his outstretched arms, "We are meant to never be heard from again." She lost consciousness.

"...The General Security Service employs administrative detention for security threats to the State of Israel...threats undermining its physical existence such as terrorist activities...perceived threats to its ability to physically exist perhaps through "information leaks...And in intelligence cases there is the additional problem of disclosing the evidence, which is presumably sensitive hence the security risk and the detention in order to quell such risk, even to the accused's legal representation in order to provide an adequate defence, even to the judge who probably does not have top secret clearance to read the documents upon which to base his decision. Did anyone read the cases I assigned?" This time silence truly befell the class.

"It looks like not," responded a voice from the group.

"Could you give us a summary?"

The phone rang in the empty apartment. Immediately the machine awakened in a buzz of moving parts and flashing lights. "It's me. We just had a lecture you should've heard. Apparently the government can forcibly relocate citizens to new cozy stylish three-by-threes without word to anybody. However, the condition is that they either are murderers or spies. It doesn't fit. My brother was not a traitor. But you also can't eliminate the option that they made too many waves and faked the whole series of events themselves to escape troubles here. They were brilliant and I bet they're sitting on the other "side of the world tanning by the ocean."

"Ocean," whispers Yuli aloud recalling her resistance to tides planning to sweep her into the unknown. "I want to jump into the water." She unplugs her bedside lamp and with that blackness comes forth. A heartbeat sounds in that dark place to be guide. The journey. From that beat spews light. She nears and nears. Between them a gang of stunted devils in charcoal leather jackets.

Cognizant that she'd require her degree to decipher this one and that it's wise not to discuss with the sane midnight meetings incorporating Satan, she flicked on the television. A South African accent anchored, "In our headlines today the physicist pair who had been declared killed in a car accident a few years ago have been discovered alive and in the custody of the Israeli authorities under allegations of security breach. The spouses had been quite vocal in their accusations against the government regarding an unsafe work environment for the professionals at the husband's place of employment and since then have been held and transferred from prison to prison across the country. And in other news..."

"Yuli! Yuli! Did you hear? Tal's alive?" screamed fellow tenants through her door, excitedly beating at it with casserole-cooking, floor-mopping fists. "Turn on the TV..." Opening the door, hopping out of reach of frenzied airborne whacks swooping past her nose mistakenly continuing to aim for the reinforced plates vibrating on their hinges. Phones sounded. Friends arrived. Ecstatic grabbing and hugging everywhere. Plenty of yells, laughter, and weeping.

"I thought that's what happened," uttered Yuli.

"We know you did."

"We were convinced you had become a lunatic," responded others.

To Aram it was a blow to the ribs. In his denial he imagined them away by their own power. He could wallow in resentment of their leisure. Now it was in his face, his brother's suffering, his own selfishness. Aram had to lock the questions inside a small box and shelf it so he may continue like any other guy. He didn't desire this story. He had his own individual plan. When it unfolded he was a kid facing the draft. How to reconcile the country he served being so duplicitous? And not in general. Not to anyone. To him. Him. Stunned. To a patriot with ambition this was not the heralding of great joy. His poor brother and Tal were better actually dying than this end. Desperate for assistance, but Aram didn't have the means.

"Yuli here...Hello?...Hello?"

"So they're not lounging around the islands... What next?..."

Recognizing his voice she buzzed the building entrance. Pained he was. Two o'clock in the morning. Reassuringly, secretly aware things were being done on their behalf, she offered, "It's okay, Aram. I've got them. You be a law student. I've got them." As little information as this was he seemed satisfied, placated. He drank a cup of tea with mint leaves, steadied himself, and motor-scootered to the dorm where a half-finished paper on criminal law awaited.

Yuli promised him she had things under control. Right. She had nothing under control. Besides depleting financial resources and no social life except conversations with her apartment vegetation, it's supposed to be good for them, this was a specimen who second-guessed every cliff wondering whether today was the day to plummet. On the standard military written psych test she flunked most sections, declaring "Yes" to "I often have strange thoughts" as an example. In order to enlist the subject yet simultaneously avoid assigning her a firearm she became an unpaid nine-to-five weekday jobnik for two years in an office in central Tel Aviv. And she wore green. A choice of roads before her feet. Up to Moshav Ora is faster. Or sideswiping its meandering mountain, the final push complete with hairpin climb. A short trail dodging evergreens leads to Rubinstein's grave. Sculpted marble piano keys magnified and irregularly arranged stand watch over kilometres of natural smoothed out risings, an inspired peaceful tribute. When the only noise is your own feet treading en route on pine needles and silt, stone and concrete. When you refresh from a shaded fountain encapsulated in cemented rocks beckoning drink.

When rudely swarms upon your lone position a fleet of revving motorcycles snapping the tranquility like twigs beneath their tires. They notice you. Yuli stilled herself. As if unfazed she maintained her extended lean over the tap. Senses registered shouts, movement, exits. A handful of men quieted each other with shushing, body hits and gestures, creeping the water platform's circumference...and Yuli. They were closing in. One set of mucky boots broke ahead of the pack and pierced the core. Too late to pretend.

"To be invisible you must believe you're not there," the biker menaced in low sluggish tones. Unwashed sandpapery exterior. Gasoline odour masked in stenches of smoke, lighter fluid, and coal the hue of his jacket hide. Reflective lenses. He eerily manipulated their exchange of places and had Yuli pressing the button. "When I would find them they would've just been moved to another cell and the search would begin again," swallowing a cold mouthful.

"Why the public declaration of their live status?"

"To keep it that way." And with that the burly figure slithered a casual retreat. His entourage followed, and they were again quickly slimily cavorting in the close of the convention of goons.

She took cue and shuffled in the trees past eyeshot homeward. Lesson of the drunk in the forest. Tal had preached that no matter how randomly the sot was bandied about rebounding off trunks like a pinball he would emerge out the far end of the maze on the same trajectory he was on when he had entered.

Chapter Three

The university was a rejuvenating locale for Aram and although his career had progressed in résumé-style ferocity past the faculty on to politics he eagerly reclaimed his old haunt in passionate sessions with the professors to codify criminal sentencing. To legalists it was imperative that sentencing leeway be removed from the hands of judges who unduly imposed minimal punishment because in existing law no minimum punishment, only a maximum, was prescribed. A codification would in essence be a large book listing all the laws, each law then listing every relevant circumstance which called for additional severity or leniency in punishment along with its resulting punishment under each circumstance to be administered exactly. No judicial discretion.

Another reason for loitering on campus when he headed one of the two most powerful parties in the knesset was Maliya. As he parked one day where the buses u-turn, preparing to jog up the mound and hurtle between the buildings to his meeting, the creature there stood at the summit entranced by the vista which stretched east until it touched Jordan. He paused to ponder her and turned to front the spectacle himself. A landscape of whitish sandy bumps mostly uninhabitable. Then he returned to her, copper-haired, dancing the breeze to detour herself as obstacle. It was the attitude, that she would toy with the wind that way through her shirt. Aram leapt closer to his destination which coincidentally neared her effecting Maliya's snapping from serenity and whipping to confront the potential menace intrusion...who was lovely...eyes softening blue...melting...unpeeling his soul and she entered. Being probably the only Maliya in Israel she was easily spotted in the school register including contact information, so Aram was only a couple of humorous comments from an invite for them to sit on that same grassy post and partake of the view together.

"For eighteen years I harboured contempt for this very scenery as the poison sea which clutched the spirit both dead and later, I discovered, living of my brother Gadi."

"How romantic. Myself, I feel the desert be my birth. To breathe clean dry winds and be free. But your venomous snake..."

"Poison sea."

"Same thing...is just as good." She knew how to do that, care for the man but compartmentalize and disengage from those mines that would trap him.

Egotism of the artist. "There's much philosophy in physics, but I wouldn't know. My parents forbid science."

Aram was taken aback.

"Too dangerous." Arms fluttering over to there, "Poison..."

"...sea."

"Don't inform them I sneak to Givat Ram and monitor classes." Her mischievous streak bare, Maliya reclined into the lawn.

"What's your physical philosophy?" Aram probed, tending toward her.

"There's something about a man, a woman, and resonance."

Good answer. It was a revelation to this beautiful burdened man that his personal tragedy impacted the existence of the free spirit laying beside him. At every turn she was more and more. Red hair in the sun, then an alabaster complexion framing green eyes one could only plunge into with abandon to find she would do the same. Not only intelligent but sincerely fascinated with the subject Gadi inspiringly instructed him as a teen. She had him at ease while not allowing his suffocation in despair. And more. There was fire. She was a tad younger. Such fire. She had the smile of an angel, but he knew she was not. He was the most wanted man in Israel. He only wanted her.

Maliya sensed his strong presence encompassing. She gave in. Secure. Excitingly terrifying. The attraction. She desired cancel space between her and this male with such vigor. His words vibrated through her from that sculptured jaw whose thoughts completed the ones in her mind. Daylight highlighting a tinge of blonde...and the eyes, his open heart, penetrating, receiving...

"Would you like to go somewhere with me?"

"Yes."

Aram promptly rose, aerating suit jacket, and collected Maliya to her feet with one still-muscular military-trained arm in a singular continuous gesture drawing her into partial hug where he focused her past his pointing finger, his shoulder pressed to her cheek. "That's my car."

Pausing. Inhaling. She slapped his abdomen, "You're it," and scurried to be first down the stairs to the lot.

He, of course, raced after.

They drove the short route and on the upbeat presented in unison, "On the Hilll of the Am-mu-niii-tion!" replete with "doo doo doo"'s and drumming. A catchy tune befitting the landmark bunker pivotal to a bloody Jordanian-Israeli war. Onward, skirting

Jerusalem's last chunk on a winding wooded road, descending her extremely steep pendulum-swing main entrance, deadly and gorgeous. Onward, zooming the flats, lush fertile farmlands, toward the coast.

"Breathing free? Or do you prefer arid pious harshness to the hedonism of the water-peoples in ancient times?" Aram quipped.

"Hey, I come from here. You're the one writing scriptures in caves of Jerusalem stone. Have you revolutionized our nation as we know her?"

"I'm working on it."

"I'll bet you..."

"Do you know that it's mandatory by law, covering your home with that expensive white-grey water-spongeing rock?"

"It reflects the city gold in sunset."

"What's your take on the subsurface platform idea for the Kinneret so Christian pilgrims can walk on water like Jesus?"

"Uh, about on par with the Western Wall's fax to G-d campaign."

"So you're not opposed to lobster in principle?"

"Principal, sidekick, garlic butter. It's all a festive Shabbat on the fire."

"How do you find my witty conversation?"

"You'd better be fantastic in bed."

"Oh, I never have sex with women with whom I engage in sarcastic banter."

"That's okay. I didn't much like talking with you anyway."

He pulled into rather a dive on a similarly quaint dilapidated wharf in Yaffo, declaring, "Don't be discouraged by its appearance. Kashrut's got nothing on these crustaceans, and I'm a good Jewish boy."

"That's not what I heard."

"Best of all, it's private."

True, there was not a mêlée to be had, only the gracious smiles and exuberant handshaking of the owner who after recognizing Aram and participating in friendly greetings all around assisted him in transplanting a simple table and chairs set to a cozy spot outside where the waves washed the dock underfoot. They dined on seafood succulently roasted. The surf beat with each morsel. They rehydrated via two sweating cans of ice cold virgin black beer.

"Walk with me, Maliya," Aram asked with upturned palm outstretched to her.

She accepted his hand and he led her along the shore. This closeness was tantalizing and every so often each's grip would tighten in enjoyment until they reached a secluded sandy patch. There nestled inside a nook between hovering crag above and vicious currents laterally they stopped. They faced each other. And then their mouths met. Entangled in tentative firm embrace. He drew her in and she pressed against him. Their lips and tongues pleasuring with a hunger. Exploring a lover excites as uncovering a new world. They dropped to their knees and sat and continued to kiss and touch and Maliya was in his lap, her legs wrapped around him. Over time the tide encroached upon their narrow enclave and they were forced to flee with perilous immediacy ascending a ramp to the apex of the crag where they sealed that afternoon in a lingering mental photograph of the sea below, aqua west to the horizon whereupon it became sky.

"Will you be with me this weekend, Maliya? We'll travel further north until it's quiet and grab a place on the Med." Aram's fingertips nudged her red hair ever so slightly behind her ear. Maliya. Maliya. "Maliya," he whispered, cradling her head in his hands.

Her eyes shut and she smiled, "I'm there."

By the time the two had returned the countryside had become slathered in pitch. Crowded

Jerusalem was alight, however, so a lofty vantage point in the centre of town which made the city seem a scattering of pinhead bulbs was Aram's destination. The real territory from this height truly resembled the miniaturized replica artfully constructed and laid on the ground beside them, if you discount of course the man-made version's large temple in the middle.

The next days achingly anticipated Aram and Maliya's liaison, its culmination in impassioned lovemaking which recessed solely to replenish exhausted bodies with the necessities of life, not that the lovers didn't consider this one of them. All week he had been calling to tantalize, describing in meticulous detail how he would delight her with a tongue that would roam every surface of her skin, fingertips barely making contact, methodically doing the same. She was not disappointed. He fervently massaged her from head to sole of foot. Enraptured. He had a stamina lasting hour upon hour. She radiated an intense satiated satisfaction. How else could he be with her? She inspired him. And she learnt by his example that what pleased her would offer same to him, and she wanted be the one that would send him to those heights. And she was successful. He, elated. It was a prime locale, as Aram had envisioned. Amid their breaths and groans they guested the churning of the sea through open windows. A cross-breeze highwayed through this vacation home along their bare wet selves, occasionally tunneling the small space between stomachs when they parted. It was day and it was night and it was day again. They did not care. Eventually they were too tired to move anything but their vocal cords.

"How was university this week?"

"I handed in a two-page assignment that was supposed to be only a dense one and a half."

"Sussita!"

"What? Anyway, the TA drew a thick red line at the page-and-a-half mark and coincidentally lost the ability to read right there, missing all my closing arguments."

"Albeit a pinch before your time, the Sussita was what happened when Israelis thought that instead of importing they would design and manufacture their own native-brand car. Wait. It gets better. Made of fiberglass, in a collision it would crack, splitting completely in two. Today you can see them abandoned in fields, being chewed on by camels."

"You're a very supportive mate."

"Don't take it to heart. I'm this close to becoming the next Prime Minister of Israel and when I walk across the freshly sponged marble in my own "parliament the cleaner can still yell at me to get off her floor."

"When the President of the United States stayed at the hotel in our neighborhood and umbrellaed our street with roadblocks, security checks, and barricades we regarded him as a mere nuisance."

"So does most of America."

Their laughter was revitalizing.

Chapter Four

Maliya would be the last in a string of affairs hitherto dissociating Aram from his authentic self which for a man of many accomplishments strangely was a giant unknown, certainly differing from the existence he readily conjured. She was simply and inexplicably a match, but what to do about his wife?

Aram's spouse passively agreed to his philandering ways in favour of remaining his spouse no matter the cost while Aram's compromise regarding the marriage was essentially not to be in it. And it was more complicated. The union had shared a promise of normalcy and stability in due course wiped out by the real anxious burden of Gadi's plight. At once bound and torn enduring hardship. Omitting that, were the spouses a good couple? He didn't know. She stayed. He stayed. That was the extent of their answer and there had been no need to further question. Now perhaps there was. He wasn't clear why this situation was different and didn't know what the outcome would be. When in doubt, defer to the status quo. Coups seek a cause and incur casualties.

As for Aram's wife, she had reason for insecurity. Despite the other women her position in society by means of her husband was assured. Of late, however, he was not hers even in name. And the one mitigating factor available to all females for her was not an option. Again, Gadi. Aram was becoming more and more remote, a feat she barely thought possible. He was not responding as he usually had. There was a distinct chance he would leave her this time. Now she asked for a baby.

"No." He saw the word exit his lips, in his imagination standing beside himself, and when it processed he understood. He had made his decision, the one he had no intention of making, but it was done. Standing there, looking at her, he remembered he loved her once. He just couldn't recall how that felt. Aram left their house and did not return.

Thirty-six. He was the age of Gadi at the moment all their lifelines irreparably splintered. A fitting time to end his marriage. Young Maliya would have been just a babe the year of the vicious abduction. He might have introduced her to Yuli, but it would have been too cruel a reminder. He refrained. Nevertheless uncanny though, Maliya's age. Perhaps she was for Aram an awakening, that he may inherit the future his brother never had. Gadi was now, well, older. Had he not been in jail he would be verging on eligibility for retirement, pension. Tal was six years younger than he, not quite the sizable gap between Aram and Maliya. They were captive the most fruitful years of their existence. Earlier, you're still searching for who you are. Afterwards, it's too late.

Not quite, apparently. A Kabbalist who had been harmlessly stalking Maliya had proffered the advice as she was rushing about town complaining of an abundance of homework and a shortage of hours that in the phrase "I don't have enough time" the word "time" should be interchanged with "life" and then the entire sentiment restated.

Dear Maliya replied to him with, "That's another thing I hate about Jerusalem," and walked away. Secretly she thought it was neat, everyone being a sage, though it's good policy not to encourage the town mystics. Moreover, she rathered toy with them, negating their clairvoyant abilities when she knew they were right. They would declare supposed facts about her which she would vehemently deny merely to deflate confidence so they would not be so quick to insinuate themselves pesteringly upon vulnerable women. It was after all her moral duty, to undermine and confuse. All those prophets thus mistied in self-doubt wandering aimlessly in the capital would be her doing.

Division was also prevalent throughout the country. Pro-peace. Pro-conservativism. Meanwhile the Territories were afire in bullets. In Aza Arabs under self-rule at their own request were drinking saltwater from the sea. Their schools closed, having no money to pay teachers. But Palestinian police had salaries and new uniforms. This situation was not conducive to easing tensions. A national election was called in Israel, Aram on the ballot. When the population set to bed voting night a win was announced for the incumbent. By morning the predicted count had tilted to Aram as leader of the new coalition government.

"Congratulations, Prime Minister!" jubilated Aram's aide and dependable friend Ben.

Aram bear-hugged and backslapped him into his office and shut the door. "Get my brother out of prison."

"I didn't hear that. So this is the plan."

"Pull strings. Make a deal."

"It'll cost you your job of all of three hours. And what colour would you like your coffin? Mucking about with the intelligence service."

"Throw them in the hold of a boat, to anywhere. I'll pay cash, favours. It doesn't matter "how."

"That's treasonous."

"My family is not."

"Maybe so. I know. Truthfully, it's doubtful even you can do it, even from here. At the very least I can wangle improvements in conditions, their treatment. You see, that presupposes working within the system and not against it. That can be done."

"Yes, that's much better," Aram remarked facetiously.

"Only with me. No discussions of this sort with anyone else." Ben shook off his noticeable agitation from their conversation before leaving the room so no well-wisher would query him. He was more adept than was conveyed by appearance.

Yuli and Scary Eyes were equally elated with Aram's promotion. Relatives of the Prime Minister were less likely to be summarily executed.

Aram's cell phone vibrated. "Yes."

"Hey, Beautiful. Sensational show."

"Maliya! Say, what's the difference between a mathematician and a physicist?"

"Stop drinking coffee and go to bed."

"The mathematician will tell him in twenty

"years."

Unfortunately, the problem with discarding very small quantities as insignificant compared to much larger components of an equation is that in impatient prioritizing and simplification the throwaway pieces just might be of paramount importance to someone else, someone who'll then meticulously, agonizingly grapple to understand the true meaning of the cancellation for decades to follow. Ben snagged Aram mid-chuckle. "Is that Maliya?"

He nodded, altering his face at Ben's grimness.

Ben mimed disconnecting a land line handset through contact with a tabletop receiver.

"Gotta go, Love. Ben is edgy. You may be on his list. Bye."

Needless to say, his aide did not appreciate the mentioning of his name, his mental state, nor the execution reference in light of the news he was prepared to deliver.

Again they made for a cloistered area. Aram held up his arms in a gesture the equivalent of "What?".

"Your girlfriend is Shabak."

Nervous laughter and disbelief were his initial sleep-deprived reactions. "You're not serious, Ben. What is this based on?"

"If you must know, as I was prostituting myself with the secret service for you as promised - they now have five-star accommodation by the way, truly comfortable - a report came in from the background check I had ordered merely as a precaution. There can be no surprises to mar the government. Of that sort. Well, lo and behold Maliya was red-flagged. Her Uncle Ofer is an operative, a bit of a rogue actually."

"But not her."

"She could be a plant. An enchanting girl who happened to have caught your eye, out of thousands. What do you know about her, her family? Per chance, how did you meet? Is she conveniently all you ever wanted? Your family has a security history. You are poking about Gadi's affairs. You, in the Prime Minister's Office. This is bad."

He was right. Aram was trampled. No coincidence.

Unmoved by her lover's shock, impish glee overtook Maliya when she heard the gossip. She was heir to a parallel to royalty in the topic of evil. How scintillating. "I always targeted him for a back-stabbing crook. I don't know why, something in the expression, unreadable, as if behind it a wall, and hiding beyond that his soul. Theoretically a person "with that measure of disjointedness could be capable of anything. My mom's fearful of him, her own brother, to the extent that he has the authority. She pays heed when he's being protective of me. But he stays afar. I don't see him much." She came across innocent.

And he believed her.

Chapter Five

Not an agent, full stop. Agent provocateur. Uncle Ofer possessed one healthy bank account and no real job to substantiate it. Pastimes include disguising himself as Border Patrol, forming mock checkpoints, and beating up Arabs. The army denied soldiers in the area of the assaults. But he was not army. He was rumored to have boarded at the home of an Israeli who went berserk and maniacally rampaged and massacred Palestinians praying at a mosque. Inciter, agitator. And he worked the other side. Anti-Israeli hate literature was disseminated in the Territories in Arabic by his hand. His superiors had him perpetuate a war, reason unknown. Yet for all his transgressions he miraculously escaped legal consequences, criminal liability. Code-named Rimon: Pomegranate...Grenade. As of late, Ofer was subjugating religious university students, instigating them into a revolutionary cult created and run by himself. Yet to be determined was whether it was actually functional or a publicity stunt aimed at deluding the populace as to the true extent of political division in the land. Hand cam footage of the participants flaunted on national television would point to the latter. Curious, though.

Then there was the incident of Gadi and Tal. Grenade was in profoundly. Only then he wasn't Grenade, rather Seed, and his team's operation was rooted in protecting state secrets in the nuclear industry. The physicists were too vocal. Their enflaming recitations on the subject of rampant disease and illness could possibly have the world believing Israel's nuclear energy production was a façade for arms manufacture when Israel would not confirm its occurrence. Seed was then a newcomer and this was not his file, per se, but his handler's. That stated, valuable contributions were made on his part for which he later was rewarded the greater autonomy evident in his successive creepy enterprises.

"The greater picture" might easily be their motto. Sacrificing quality of life to annex strategic parcels of land, for to conquer territory you must put people on it regardless of the fact they periodically get bombed and their children must sleep in bunkers. Propagating a war devastating economies, psyches, tossing lives, so that...so...Explanations elude. Perhaps so as not to settle individual property claims which could strip a small country. Censoring sensitive information from society which would frighten them from their enemies and health hazards, demoralize, convey their powerlessness amidst bureaucratic corruption, to keep them complacent, enlisting, and residing in numbers in the state. And what of forming a rival terrorist organization in order to infiltrate those circles, which de facto increased efficiency in the newly competitive market of subversion? Not to forget their radical group also monstered out of control becoming yet another opponent. Someone was on the ball the day that idea was conceived.

Had Aram uncovered Grenade's part in his brother's disappearance Maliya may not have seen twenty-one. His history as Seed was well buried.

Yuli's man hadn't revealed the connection to specific parties responsible, either, and he was entrenched in the underworld. Thus the secrecy. His place and contacts had to remain solid for him to be effective in his work. Green Eyes teetered the fine line, that way he didn't have to make up his mind. Word trickled down to him about his subjects' new digs and that it took some manipulation. He encoded the message into an Old City religious pamphlet on the Zohar. Yuli, relieved, knew it had to have been Aram. He had risen and amassed power and was using his influence. She had thought him lost. She was wrong.

Grenade also was informed of renewed interest in his old case with indications it travelled straight up to the Prime Minister's Office. He was hurriedly reassigned Seed and granted full authority to close the gaping hole he in part had left. Eighteen years is a considerable period, though, and seasoned Grenade was no longer protégé Seed. The situation was detained citizen intellectuals. The problem was high level interference potentially exposing and embarrassing intelligence operations and operatives responsible. Essentially there were just three options, everything else imaginative methods of carrying them out. One, do nothing. Consequences centre on public scrutiny and interference and future uncertainty depending on the pressure exerted. He may have to take further actions as countermeasures later on as the situation merited. Two, set them free. Pardon, deportation, threats, identity switch. Any was ripe for implementation. Intervention ceases on their behalf. But then their focus will change. It will be directed toward him. Three, they could be killed. Questions, inquiries would arise. All ties and informants could be silenced and then it all, being an academic exercise, would eventually end. Number three was the messiest and most dangerous careerwise but it would effectively quash all opposition and finish the matter. On the other hand, the first two carried better legal ramifications for him. He hadn't killed anybody yet. Despite political heat he would keep his job. These two options meant, though, that this was ongoing. The parties would keep after him until satisfaction set in. So, offensive moves by him would be needed to put them on the run and be a defensive strategy quelling future repercussions. He went to pay a visit.

Gadi and Tal would be released. When told by this scoundrel they were numb and distrusting. They'd be declared escapees and be shot.

"Relax. I've just been put in charge. I've made my decision and came to tell you myself. You won't walk out with me now. Paperwork, signatures, a couple of days. The case is high priority direct from the Prime Minister, your brother." Seed addressed Gadi. "That's how this came to be all of a sudden. Meanwhile, please be patient. You'll receive celebratory meals, exquisite food, to buy us time to prepare documents and contracts for you to sign as conditions of your reprieve. You will keep a low profile, no demonstrations, rantings against the government. Standard clauses. You've been in prison, but we have dirty faces and need to show a semblance "of cleanliness. We need protection from backlash. Wait it out and try to understand." He shook their limp hands and exited like a man with plenty to do. After all, Grenade still had a civil war to formulate. This old business was a major inconvenience.

Gadi and Tal absorbed the legitimacy of the briefing. Worried was the leadership about its appearance. Papers to sign. "Eighteen years should have taught us how to be quiet. Okay?" Gadi insinuated.

"If he had left the door unlocked I'd have remained here." Tal was still traumatized. The time lapse between the news and its fruition was necessary. "He's new, he says. Aram is definitely new as leader of the government. The upgrade must be thanks to him. Now, freedom. Your little brother did it. Did he?"

"They're not as confident as usual. Aram has undermined that, and they're folding," Gadi continued in the vein of Tal's analysis.

"And he came in person...?"

"To check us out, make sure we had settled down and would comply. Maybe he is new. Maybe he's just a new face, an excuse for policy change and pressure exerted upon them."

"He's a liar," sniffed Tal.

"Yes, but the message might be true. It is after all their style, clothing the truth in a gigantic lie."

Waves and waves of appetizers, entrées, desserts, poured into their enclosure. Chocolates, fruits, wine. Plates everywhere. Gadi requested his captors eat samples before he and his wife which they were very willing to do and with no ill effects. A good omen was it that the sassy jailers believed the judgement rescinded, so Gadi and Tal dined. There was nothing wrong with the food, not a kitchen germ. They'd have to learn to lower their guard in the outside world. Things would be different.

At the far end of the complex Seed marched in, arms loaded with files spewing dog-eared papers. "The transfer is now," he ordered as handfuls of agents kept pace with him down the hall and stairs. He told the regular staff to enter and clear all the plates and so forth. He and his hand-picked group hung back. Then they went in. "You're transferring now," he reported to Gadi and Tal as he dropped the files onto the table in their abode. Agents were everywhere in the close space, familiar faces, Seed, others winding around in the shadows. The regulars were actually picking up kitchenware as Seed's junta enveloped the two prisoners and injected them. This time, unlike the last when he knocked them out, they wouldn't wake up in jail. A reverse journey. Path of least resistance.

Ben received word and notified Aram. "Gadi's overseers have recently informed me the case was overturned and the two have been moved. They're being let go."
"Where are they now?"
"We're not sure."

Yuli shot up in bed and awoke.

Sleepless night for all.

A Bedouin had seen the flame. He approached without sound in the moonlight and for hours crouched on a hill. A bonfire. Men. The smell. A funeral pyre. Sense of déjà vu. It had been many years.
Dawn. Yuli opened her door to...he was large and filthy and said nothing...close the door...close the door!...he dipped his glasses and braced the metal against his arm as it was shutting. Emerald Eyes! She pulled him in. They stood there scrunched in the hallway between her little rooms as he recounted in precise detail the murders of Tal and her husband. The

façade. Fatal injection. Worst of all returning their corpses to the original crash site and charring them to simulate death in the past explosion and decomposition of nearly two decades. As if they had been there all along.

"Zmam!" Yuli screamed in a whisper. "Evil. Conspiracy."

They had been reliably I.D.'d by sources right to the burning. It was them.

"The news broadcast they'd been hostages of the government. Everyone will learn what they've done."

"The Israeli public will believe what they're told. The news made a mistake. Their source was incorrect. I told the news they were political prisoners. I'm the kook. No one will think anything other than they died in the crash ages ago."

"A funeral." Yuli was hardly lucid.

"You don't know any of this. There was no investigation. They've been dead forever. Do not have a funeral, or you may be in it."

An elaborate rouse created in attempts of hoodwinking every single person into its web. Freedom, it seems, was a relative term.

"Should you need to contact me, write verse containing the words 'summer snow' in the "classifieds. I like poetry."

"What of...?"

"It's over. That trail has been cold since we met. Remember, there were only two bodies. Stay away. Don't make it three."

Sentences raced before her face. They're dead. Was he still here? Two bodies. No, he was not.

Red-eyed Aram, afoot on parliamentary ground, again posed his question to Ben.

"Security has its own agenda."

Chapter Six

Gadi's second death drove Aram into an abyss of misery from which himself he could not extricate. He had been on the outs with Maliya over her being the niece of a spook, a fact over which she certainly had no control. Ben had even attempted to mediate although he had the most reservations about their coupling, explaining that amongst security operatives themselves lateral factions are unaware of each other's actions. Chains of command run vertically. If Maliya was plainly a civilian Ofer's movements were utterly camouflaged to her, and with dissension brewing in the country the aide had more pressing issues than one girl easily not responsible for all the wrongdoing of the entire secret service. Was this going to be his marriage revisited?

Ultimately Aram had a sense that he was the cause. If he could close his eyes and cease for what he had done.

His heart begged for Maliya and his rage dissipated. And he gave himself over to her love, otherwise he was destroyed. She, she had him back. His absence had been crushing. They had such need. Relinquishing to the fervor they were ready to adventure each other, so sloughing off the world they retreated to their favorite coastal nest and dared be happy. Maliya was not one to cower in despair and be victim of hurt. She surrendered to joy and the immediacy of relishing Aram, her idol. He was obsessed with her.

"Are you a concept or calculations man?" Maliya was glad to return to that sharp mind of Aram's. Skyward she was elevated, past the palm trees and ice cream.

Aram celebrated Gadi and his Tal as he pondered which type of physicist layman he was.

"Do you play with difficult philosophy until the solution becomes more easily accomplishable or do you receive as is the intricate ideas you are given and proceed methodically to tackle a subsequently longer set of robotic tasks?" she elaborated.

Aram chose one.

Maliya, the other.

"The danger with not dealing with logic as it is presented is that when switching the parts around they must truly be interchangeable. Erroneous assumptions will warp the outcome and it will never be correct."

"But sometimes merely doing what is demanded is nearly impossible or extremely time-consuming at best."

"However, you're closer to getting it right, even if you should fail."

Maliya started imitating the low-pitched incomprehensible hum of a rowdy classroom, signalling her mate to grab for her and initiate tickling and wild animal growls and howls as she screamed playfully. Sex interspersed with running and dancing on the beach and romping in the waves, lobster and more sex. He held onto her so she would not let him go. They reclaimed each other in tender caresses and probing gaze. Aram made love to Maliya slowly. Almost painful being so content. He drank the beauty of the moment and tears streamed down his cheeks and over his nose like a little cliff and she took them into her sweet open mouth, salty like the sea. And the one dripping softly over his nose her tongue plucked as if stealing a treasure before someone noticed and he would smile and then he would laugh and blissfully engulf her mouth in his. Then the wrapping of their limbs around each other and the penetrating of their body parts into each other would all begin again.

"Did you really consider me a spy for Uncle Ofer?" she spoke quietly between light kisses.

"Maliya," Aram's lips occupied, he narrowly missed expelling the sentiment. "As long as you use your powers for good I wouldn't care anymore."

"Well I'm not, but I like those powers."

"You...possess exquisite...powers." Aram carried her from one corner of the bed to the other in illustration.

"Aaa!" she mocked protest. Copulating. Repositioning. "There, I've done it. I have overthrown the government and you never predicted it," she declared, straddled atop him.

"Ah, my queen...I submit."

She bent down to reach his face with hers and they tumbled across the disheveled bedding.

"But I never forgot it was my throne first," Aram interjected as she descended into a giggly commoner alongside him.

In Jerusalem Yuli was on a shopping escapade in the open market, eating shawarma en route to a scenic park where she would rest, engaging in a dialogue open forum inside her head. "You've got to admire the foresight of the man who saw a pack of wolves hunting in the wild and thought to himself 'I think I'll bring one of those into my home, feed him, and put him to sleep in a little bed. I'll groom him and purchase chew toys so he won't eat the furniture, or me, and maybe a coat.'" She chuckled aloud. People glanced with perplexed expressions at the lady sitting alone enshrouded in bags joking with herself. That couldn't be a positive sign. At least she didn't hear other voices in her inner conversations, only her own. And she still didn't carry a gun.

The one man not relishing in the delight of existence these days was Ofer. Places to go, people to kill. That must have been it. He knew of the Prime Minister and his niece and was agitated.

Yuli dreamt once more. In a chamber. Air thinning. Freezing to death. The skull-demon in the ice water would steal her beloved dog. Yuli didn't have a dog. Two bodies. There were three. Where was Tali's infant? Not even they would have killed someone so young. Time-bomb. Parents recently murdered. Would they go after a child that grew into adulthood to resemble them? Urgency. Two corpses. Don't make it three. Stay away. Virtual duplicate of the parents. Tali, my Tal. Save the baby. No longer a child. Was that why the murders?

Aram had outright refused to have a child with his first wife. She complied. And then she had mentioned it in desperation. It was a blade through him.

Maliya's parents were also aflutter about a child, their child, and the turn of events. They had been receiving counsel from Ofer regarding her relationship of which she had failed to inform them with one older leader of the country, ladies' man, divorcé, whose family had been in trouble with the law. He omitted the section where they were decent professionals whom he attempted to slay in their car along with their baby, kidnapped and caged under dubious legal pretenses, stealing the baby, later murdering them and covering his handiwork, baby's fate unknown. That was irrelevant. She was to keep away from this man. Characteristically, Maliya succumbed to their influence and was repentant for her young girl's infatuation having been so naïvely misdirected as to have caused her parents worry. Appreciative of their wise advice she would obey it, insomuch as she did every other directive.

"Aram!"

"What are you doing right now?"

"Writing a poem, about you. It starts:

> His eyes are still soft for me
> body wanting more
> searching hands grasping...

"Maliya, I can't presently."
Smirks of innuendo all around.
She continued:

> ...out mute words
> darkness breathes of him
> a wave envelopes me
> turn 'round he's there.

"And since you're into interruption you'll only get one stanza tonight."

"Aw, it sounded hot, too. Enough about you, I'm on the podium tomorrow."

"Tell me."

"I'm for expanding codification..."

"...that doesn't exist..."

"Correct...to security issues and to establish paragraphs as crimes of result rather than action."

"So you could only jail a snitch after the country's gone."

"Similar to homicide."

"That would eliminate the conundrum of one man's leak being another's informing the public based upon interpretation of the perpetrator's motives..."

"...because the crime would depend on what in

"fact happened with the information disseminated. The damage together with the motivation determines the prohibition to be enforced."

"Now who's stomping the system's toes? You're gonna make a lot of friends with this one, Aram."

"It's one matter sinking to the tactical depths of your enemies to combat them."

"You can't philosophize to a knife, gun, or bomb."

"But there's a world between that and silencing legitimate differences of opinion. Do you know it is permissible to implement mild torture during interrogations?"

"Isn't that an oxymoron? As long as it's mild. I for one rather my torture mild."

"And what if the interrogator's interpretation is akin to the cook's at that Indian restaurant we frequent?"

"So what do the rest of the western countries do?"

"They don't write it down."

Chapter Seven

The political situation in the country was rapidly deteriorating. A peace accord with the Palestinians had brought more unrest and violence as factions vied for power in the Territories and they attempted to establish rule. Israelis were more nervous than usual with the events that transpired since relinquishing control of those areas. And the religious right wing was threatening to dissolve the coalition and topple government leadership. As if that would not suffice, the Shin Bet also had a schedule. Grenade's staged revolt would be backdrop to a plot centred on Aram, his greatest undertaking yet.

Ben was in grave character, comparative to his normal disposition which was morose at best. "I'm assigning you a police guard."

Aram was unmoved.

"I'm hearing things, dissension. Your safety is involved."

"Is this absolutely necessary?"

The aide found Aram lacking reluctance to the idea. For him this behaviour equalled full out compliance. Perhaps he too possessed a measure of fear.

Epitomizing bad timing the American president returned. Security contingent unprecedented. Forces were arranged as multiple layers of rinds surrounding a fruit. Army was outer shell, working well on a large perimeter. Then police, controlling traffic and civilian movement. Farther inside, within actual buildings containing him, Israeli Secret Service. And in the core, American Secret Service. When he was on the go everything else stopped, limiting the variables of the equation to a minimum. Aram had his policeman.

Grenade was grooming a less aged accomplice who had been shuttled back from the Eastern Bloc with thumbs up critique. Not keeping a low profile he was the setup, willingly, on the payroll, this guy also a member of Grenade's loud splash university kid religious revolt group.

Anew were transmitted to Ben's antennae rumblings much disquieting. There was plotted a hit. He implored Aram to wear a vest.

A call from the head of the Shabak was placed to Aram directly. They conversed, the two, in person about the state of mayhem both inside and over the Green Line and his responsibility to the current government in light of his appointment as chief by Aram's men. Shabak elite had been formulating a plan whereby the Right's anti-peace stance will be shamed into becoming mute and the PM's leadership will retain the strength needed to enact the accord. And this is advantageous to security because the sooner the transfer of power is completed matters in the Territories will settle, as well as the fact that should the government topple so too will his role as chief. How the plan benefits Aram is obvious. He will make history. Oh yeah, and the concept entailed one small simulated assassination attempt, which is what Aram was already hearing albeit unfortunately as real. Much regrets for the fright. Although that also confirmed the operation was going well.

Aram, weathered by his history with these... couldn't fathom the workings of their minds. A fake assassination?

"Yes! That's the beauty of it."

Adrenaline junkies trained to kill. That was the problem. Just a game to them.

Knowing Aram's personal affairs the chief name-dropped Ofer as someone who could be trusted who was on ground level of the operation.

The real motivation behind this scenario was anyone's guess. Should intelligence be against the peace process they truly could stop it by shows of civil disobedience and a re-election, that being more their style. Purporting to do it all for the pro-peace regime but carrying it out backwards was just odd, also strangely in keeping with their modus operandi. Perhaps security functions best in the midst of chaos, a third option, for there the future is whatever security would have it be.

Aram related to Ben his talk with the intelligence chief word for word.

Puzzled, Ben studied the carpet. And then he looked to Aram. Then he pondered the upholstery some more. "You're keeping the guard," pointing at him as if ready to add some crucial piece of data which he was just short himself of comprehending before he went away.

Discuss it did Aram a third time, now with Maliya, whose radar detected something amiss at the mention of Ofer. She had not told her lover of the family's problem with their relationship, until then, an omission which together with Aram's news might have amounted to a bullet. However, Aram had learnt the most effective method for foiling secret plots: tell everyone. It gathers information, good samaritans, and witnesses. Maliya offered number one, the information that Ofer was not a friend of the couple. That someone else in the net might aid them from the inner circle was number two. Lastly, should a vile plan go through, that people would at the very least learn the truth would be three.

Ofer may very well have been scheming a privately orchestrated series of events on his own time, aside from the chief of intelligence's orders, but so was Ben. The more digging he did the more disturbing he found the facts. Aram was in trouble. All were enemy. It was his sole option.

"You're worse than them," the Prime Minister accused his aide.

Maybe. Ben would counter the Shabak's fake assassination with a veritable escape under the umbrella of the former. They should also be prepared if by the way the attempt suddenly turned real.

"So I flee. Where do I go? What do I do?" Aram asked.

Anywhere on the globe, just spin and fly. He can take his lady love with him. "And here's how we'll do it," Ben mysteriously began. He fancied himself a sleuth as a youth and in politics he saw none of it wasted. "I have been given word from your top "spy man nonetheless that the setting will be Saturday night at the rally right down there in Sacher Garden. It'll be huge. Performances from big Israeli rock stars, free food, fireworks. Fantastic."

"Can you get to the bit where I almost die yet somehow don't?"

"Yes." The pointing finger which thought for itself returned. "They're planning to shoot you."

"A shooting?" Now it was getting a little too macabre, the foretelling of his demise.

"All fake." His other digits joined the first outstretched one in a dismissive wave as he came back on track.

"Where?"

"In Sacher Garden."

Aram grimaced angrily at him. That was not what he meant.

"So you'll hurl yourself into your car which I'll be chauffeuring...our plan...we'll pick up Maliya and I'll scoot you over to the chopper pad."

"What if they really shoot me?"

"Bulletproof vest. But let's hope it's not in the head. That would be really unfortunate."

"I'm glad you thought this through."

For the most part he had. The key was to give a semblance of obliging while remaining alert, enacting their own play, and uncovering further details on Ofer since they had his name. Now he was under perpetual surveillance and would reveal the nature of the operation. He betrayed too much. Ofer's stranglehold on his sister, Maliya's mother, and his unhealthy influence relating to matters involving Maliya interested Ben. Maliya's father also in tow. If Ofer was such a bad character why not be done with him? What power did he have over them?

Now, Maliya. Uncle Ofer knowing the assassination plot was in progress was not keen on her acquaintance with the PM. Understandable. Or was he after Aram anyway? Aram was a target. Perhaps Ofer was just the marksman. Maliya, Maliya had something important to offer. She was the go-between even if it was not pre-planned. Had the affair been staged Maliya and Ofer were a team. If the girl was not supposed to be in the mix she constituted a gigantic disruption. She was the soft spot to Uncle Ofer. Ben needed to comb through every detail of her history and note the outstanding feature, reminiscent of Torah analysis as a boy. When a letter was written in larger type or with superfluous design flares, or with repetition of words, attention was drawn to convey some particular importance, the accent itself seeming silly and inconsequential but divulging an idea of major importance in the commentary. That's it! How did he not spot this before?

Chapter Eight

"Why didn't you tell me your Maliya was adopted?" Ben posed to Aram.

"I didn't know, and I suspect neither does she, the manner in which she rambles on about their similarities and discrepancies personalitywise as though she's analysing genetic transference through the generations."

"Do you know she's from outside the country?"

"Hello, I'm to be done in tomorrow. That my woman may be a far-travelled gentile is the least of our woes."

"Not necessarily. The transaction deals with an orphanage in Russia. Not exactly a modern filing system. Untraceable."

"Of course."

"Which means it could have been fake."

"So she's not a kibbutznik after all," Aram joked, alluding to the socialism of the original settlement movement. "Who is she, Ben?"

"Don't know. But I know who brokered the foggy business."

"Uncle Ofer!" they answered in tandem. Well, Aram answered. Ben merely liked hearing his own voice.

Ben continued, "...social services department of child welfare and development."

"When he's not snuffing me."

"Quite."

"He is the man with the connections and a pathological urge to circumvent the law. It's no surprise that he did the impossible to get his sister a baby."

"Good point."

"What exactly did he do?"

"He didn't give his sister and her husband a baby."

"And why?" Aram asked in conjunction with the first question not paying heed to the response given in between, still in his own internal symposium.

"We can't decipher from whence she came, so it is blurry why she was entered into the family portrait by Ofer. Maybe because he could assist."

"Always the philanthropist, that man."

"Maybe he had plans for her. But you're missing the best part. Whoever Maliya is she's not who the family says she is."

"What?" Aram's mind left his impending death in that instant.

"The papers have her adopted as an infant.

"The family moved during her childhood with the previous neighbours not placing her in the household at all for those years."

"Until they moved." Aram's token landed.

"And she miraculously appeared, not a newborn. Sentimental Ofer kept her real birth year. Then he backdated the adoption."

"To hide the date of transfer. When did they move? How old was she?"

"She was two. The time of your brother's disappearance."

More ashen was Aram than Ashkenazis are prone to get. Legs wavered. Body and stare were frozen.

"Congratulations Aram! This could be your missing niece. Should it be so, however, you may want to cease being lovers. It's not illegal under Jewish law but certainly frowned upon in the modern world." Ben sincerely considered the find some sort of miracle.

Aram imagined the building caving into him. His composure so severely undermined, a few more moments in this immobilized state and Ben would surely on his behalf summon a paramedic.

"I'll conduct a DNA test. Perk up sir, you're getting blown off tomorrow." And Ben slapped him on the back. "What are the chances? This worked out well, in fact." He was inferring that nabbing the missing niece and her inclusion in the imminent run was well coordinated albeit unintentional. Despite de facto familial ties the blood bond puts her in jeopardy. Her association with Aram endangers him. Could it be that it was their relationship which brought final measures upon Gadi and Tal at this date? Never would the inmates have been freed or they would have honed in on their child, and unearthed the culprit... Ofer. Obviously involved in the source operation...he handed off their daughter...he...would then have murdered to avoid the reunion...to keep Maliya... elude culpability...seal the mission file. He'd do more. Ben rushed to the girl, centre of the fury. He got the sample. To be honest his lab buddy extracted her blood, a piece of the intrigue of upcoming Saturday night. Ben wasn't much for needles, or bodily fluids, or pain. Definitely the one you'd request in a crisis.

Grenade's protégé busily prepped for the assault. His aim, perfect. He was ready to go down for the cause.

No, Grenade approved not of his niece's affair with the Prime Minister but the very fact they were carrying on suggested their ignorance of her identity, a minute detail sustaining their liveliness. Fulfilling his obligation he related to all security involved in the rally his disinformation campaign of an assassination on the PM. It was a phony. His protégé would mount the supposed attack and required access and free reign in the secure zones. He was not to be hindered or injured during the process as he is a paid operative acting on command. As per any attempted criminal act upon the PM, he is to be promptly arrested and removed into custody.

Saturday. The DNA test had not yet been completed.

Grenade handed a paper bag to his accomplice, the contents comprising of one handgun and bullets.

Aram's police guard advised him to wear the vest he had provided at that night's rally. Although others around him had relaxed their vigilance, the guard was wired for trouble. So much so, he suggested Aram cancel altogether.

Dutifully, the Prime Minister would attend, his guard's misgivings weighed and tossed, and alongside those the policeman's present of vest which would not be required. The event was a concert after all. Aram was not clear-minded. Hazy mist of reconciliation and loss.

Ben saw in Aram a man not there and worried he'd muck up the goings on. That thought got interrupted by an urgent call from the hospital. Ben's brother was in an accident, taken to emergency. "I'll check things out, see my parents. There's plenty of time between now and your funeral."

"Car accident?" Aram questioned while an ominous psychological shroud suffocated the room.

"Don't go there." Ben read him. He thought so too. "This is becoming a trend."

Maliya had not seen Aram since a wild raucous and very private Thursday evening, and morning. He sounded strange on the phone since. She could not block his tone from her every thought afterwards. Why must he do this? They could just take off without the charade. Too risky. Aram was a wreck. Ben's concept...Ben, she would have known... was to allow the intelligence service a back door, as they had previously contrived, thereby allowing the couple to leave. The Shabak could use the front any way they chose politically, and due to the fiasco with Aram's family they'd be glad to have him gone. But Aram wouldn't need to die. Great on paper.

Nonetheless she had to get into position.

The concert was broadcast live across Israel and into Yuli's living room. Yuli held her cheeks and dug her nails in. "Poor Aram," she thought aloud as it transpired. They had him on stage singing. No political future was worth that embarrassment. The Song of Peace nonetheless. Oh boy, was he in for a ribbing. Fireworks. And it was done. Next to air was the movie of the week. She quickly mixed a hot chocolate and sat in wait.

A daze of performers, music, jubilation. Aram was ushered to the limousine pickup area as colourful explosions in the Jerusalem sky dazzled the audience which remained packed before the stage. He glanced upwards at the boisterous specks and their roars took him to the coast with Maliya as lovemaking ate away the hours. Nothing was reality. They'd continue on as is and go back there. Then it happened. Gunfire. He whipped around to see a young man lunging in close proximity shooting at his torso. The limo pulled in tight. His police guard shoved him inside and tumbled on top of him himself as the car sped off, the guard scarcely in the vehicle. Security heaped on top of the shooter as yells of "Blank! Blank!" were heard.

In the car Aram lay motionless, taking inventory. He was okay. They really were blanks. This instance his family had been granted a reprieve. "I'm fine," he informed his guard who had yet to disenfranchise himself from the Prime Minister's person, strewn as they were throughout every cranny of the back seat and floor. Not believing the assailant would shoot blanks the policeman was not smiling and laughing in tense ecstasy along with Aram as he swore he was not injured. And it took some maneuvering before Aram, literally under guard, had regained enough freedom to crank his head and survey the rest of the limousine. Ben was not present. Aram could not recognize the driver. He did, however, identify Ofer by memory of the photograph in his dossier...and was struck by his hardness of face.

Grenade jammed a silencer gun into Aram's chest and fired. And again. And again. The Prime Minister visibly shook absorbing the force of the bullets into him. He bled all over the guard, shocked, prevailing upon his jellied extremities to mount an offensive directed at Grenade.

A police car sights the black limousine driving at a crawl the lightless alleys. The lone uniformed cop exits his car and walks to the other. His footsteps clanging on the pavement, he squints at the darkened windows. One rolled down half way. "Possibly to assist you?" he ventured toward no-one.

Popping an ugly jovial head out, blocking the remainder of the vehicle interior was Grenade in the back seat. "Yes, definitely, officer. Our man was shot in the arm," he told him, shifting ever so slightly so the uniform could glimpse the Prime Minister's wounded police guard unconscious beside him. "We're trying to find the hospital." They were both on top of and obliterating Aram exuding vast amounts of blood from behind the many parts of his dress suit onto the floor.

"Follow me," commanded the uniformed policeman dashing for his car, igniting the vicinity with flashing colours and sirens, escorting the royal hearse at top speed. They weren't a great distance from the central hospital and could have arrived much sooner after the preliminary concert assault had they been so inclined.

Ben was at Hadassah across town stranded in the netherworld. Sprinting through dead streets. Tearing past university dorms. National Headquarters. He'd commandeer a motorized something in there. Home of elite cops, intelligence. Continue running.

The two vehicle motorcade of marked car and government limo shot past Maliya's rendezvous point with epic drama permeating all senses. Amiss was the plan. She dipped in retreat from the avenue into the foliage on Givat Ram grounds behind a giant piece of artwork.

Yuli's movie was blurbing a Hebrew bulletin of breaking news soon to preclude the scheduled programming. It would take some time though, from source to censor to camera.

"Taxi!" hollered Ben pouncing into traffic to snare him travelling the wrong way on the far side of the barrier. "Sacher Garden for now." They u-turned through a break in the grass and rock centerpiece. Ben clutched the driver's radio from him, tearing it out of the console. "You are not in danger," he reassured him. "No communication. This is official government business. Lives are on the line. No communication until it's over. One hour. Promise me. Please. I need you to help me." Ben was panting. Ben was desperate. Ben was removing a chunk of bills from his pocket to award the stranger for his cooperation. He offered his name, raising the handful to bring it in for a landing on the seat and secure it warmly against the driver's thigh.

"Mussah," beamed Ben's impromptu emergency hour chauffeur exuberantly extending his non-steering hand for the introductions.

"Can you hurry, Mussah? But don't get detected. No police. No army. No Shabak."

The Palestinian-Israeli grunted in acknowledgment. Of the aforementioned he wasn't exactly a fan.

Ben turned the radio dial, stationing it to receive pertinent incoming transmissions. On cue the announcer apprised of crucial developments which they were poised to specify.

"Whoy, what now?" vented Mussah as they dispatched to ground zero.

Chapter Nine

Aram's limo reluctantly swept into Shaarei Tzedek, tugged in by the flatfoot. Pandemonium marred Grenade's launch as he improvised loyal servant for the hospital staff. He was not set up to play this venue. "The Prime Minister has been shot, repeatedly," he declared. "Also his guard." A flurry of medical personnel swallowed them into the building.

Amazed, this was the first the uniformed policeman heard that the incident involved the Prime Minister. "I'll call it in to secure the area," he offered Grenade.

"Yes. Thanks for all your help, officer," noting his badge number. Alone, Grenade made some back-up calls of his own.

Israel's Channel One abruptly cut their movie to deliver the report that there had been an attempted assassination on the Prime Minister and that he had been shot and was transported to the central hospital, currently undergoing treatment. Yuli jumped to where they had announced.

Meanwhile Ben's taxi was probing the surrounds of Sacher Garden to no avail when they got the radio news of Aram's revised siting and adjusted their course accordingly. Suffice it to say, Mussah was a smidgeon spooked he was on this particular trail with the stranger beside him, but obliged nonetheless.

"Turn in there," Ben requested of the driver. "Flash your beams. That's it. Again. Again." Expletive. "Wait here for me." He invaded the brush in search of her, but Maliya was gone. "To the hospital," closing his door.

She had heard on her headset and was forging a path on foot through the science campus knifing the dark straight to Aram.

The gurneys were wheeled into their respective surgeries. Aram's guard had received a bullet in the arm which went right through, having occurred from short range. Still groggy, he was regaining his faculties before the team, complaining of a headache. He'd been whacked on the temple with a hard blunt object. "That may have slowed your circulation enough to prevent further blood loss," surmised his doctor. For the moment he was cleaned, bandaged and refueled with the red stuff until a need for intensive nerve therapy could be ascertained.

Along the corridor the staff diagnosing Aram made some remarkable discoveries. Upon preliminary palpation interns had found Aram's pulse robust and rhythmically sound. Nurses were puzzled by the discrepancy between this healthy heart rate and his appearance, swimming in Maliya's blood. Until he drew up his eyelids to view them all. The surgeons intuited a necessity for a more intimate examination and so proceeded to remove Aram's outer clothing which was wired and padded and there were empty pouches attached to intravenous tubing containing hemoglobin-type residues. Then a mad beast waving his gun forced the room's occupants out. They passed his buddies on the opposite side of the door. The stern plain clothes unit of these fellows was everywhere. Grenade, too, checked Aram's pulse. In the mayhem of Uncle Ofer's entrance the patient had managed to reassemble somewhat his outer garments and once more feign dead. The beating heart unfortunately was a giveaway. Ofer could solve that. Aram heard glass smashing as the agent attacked the cabinet for his drug of choice, and then Aram rushed him before the administering of the lethal pharmaceutical. Sparring, Ofer quickly comprehended Aram's vest and squib apparatus, quietly commending him on his craft. A hubbub ensues beyond the door distracting them both as it flings open. Just a lackey in scrubs, at once no aid to Aram and no match for the man who was Seed. But he engaged in the battle to their surprise and was remarkably effective for the blood leaking from his bound arm. It was then that the two recognized him. Aram's guard drained his battery in a last ditch charge at Grenade and bid the Prime Minister fly.

Crawling with Shabak was the hospital, but to limit legal responsibility the number of men in Grenade's faction was marginal. And due to the escorting policeman's interference the unforeseen hospital sojourn was also not organized, many of Grenade's group still improperly deployed. That is how Aram snuck about, finally exiting via an unwatched passageway. Intelligence that did see him during his travels were on the other story, the fake assassination, and figured it was as per the script when he ran by. The ones truly in the know had been delayed by Aram's very busy and agile guard or simply had not yet arrived at the new scene of the crime. Wile and loyalty in the Prime Minister's camp had bought a measure of time, luck and strangers' good intentions a few ticks more.

Yuli landed upon the hospital. Word got to her that the frenzy was staged and the Prime Minister had in fact already left. She remained there, distraught.

Inspired by her presence, Grenade reformulated.

"The Prime Minister of Israel has been assassinated" read the broadcasts. "He was shot by a lone gunman before boarding his limousine just after the concert at Sacher Garden. His surgeons at Shaarei Tzedek had been unable to restore him when he was shuttled in critically wounded."

"Oh my G-d," exclaimed Mussah.

As the taxi swung into hospital territory Ben was not of the opinion recent news bode well for Aram. He eyed Yuli. This last murder was too much. Ben comforted her aloud, joining her in grief. Then he whispered under the radar, his mouth tucked very personally into her hair, "Have you seen the body?"

She retracted from him slightly, her expression widening in a spooked horse look.

He hugged her back in tight. "Let it go," Ben emoted for the benefit of the masses. "Make it convincing," he added, only for her. Questioning Yuli about Maliya the girlfriend brought a similarly surprised response. "I have to clean the office immediately," he announced. Security would expect the aide to dispose of sensitive files at such a time. So he abandoned her there. On the chance Aram was alive, Yuli's outpouring was Ofer's pawn since he had not the proper body. If she accepted a closed casket so must everyone else. And the personnel's behaviour, and artifacts littered haphazardly in the ward, and the bloody floors. None were lost on him.

Aram wandered the streets of Jerusalem dodging cars, evading lamplight. Had to reach Maliya ...Maliya his niece. He did not desire see her niece. Fortunate to have survived. In the fog of his ideals, the barriers melted wrongly and mangled. Could not face her. Yet there she was. She stood atop a hill as a shadow of illumination, surveying. Having charted her course she skittered down the side, shaving it as she slid. She had left her post and was heading for him and Ofer and whatever awaited her where she was going, it didn't matter. It didn't matter. Had to reach Maliya. He sprung forth and frightened her, just being there suddenly. Then she recognized him as her Aram and was winded again, him seeming a ghoul from a crypt. Eh, this city was built on bodies. The filthy pair clutched each other in the dust cloud they had created in the wadi.

Ben and Mussah gridded the area between the

hospital and university, as well as circular drives could be squared out and Aram had taken plenty a shortcut. The aim was to pluck survivors before somebody else did. "There. Do you see the spectres in those evergreens?" Ben pointed to lead Mussah in. "There are my bodies. Both!" That had to be them hand in hand clambering back up into the university. Honestly, Ben's stalking taxi propelled them forward at increasing velocity. "Right. I know their destination. We'll connect at the artwork in the entrance as we attempted earlier."

"I'll have to go around the long way," Mussah warned. As they circumvented the tree-lined walkways by a more passable route congestion was overtaking the area. Aside from the police blocking off a large parcel of crime scene where thousands stood at the rally, there was the secured hospital zone containing valuable information for the investigation, and now sandwiched between the two mourning countrymen were amassing in crowds at the legislature and in the streets up to it conducting candlelight vigils. It would be impossible to reach the helicopter at parliament with these developments. Moment by moment population controls were augmented.

Ben ambushed Maliya and Aram in the rendezvous shrubs previous to their making an unintentional public appearance from the afterlife. They would not have approached the taxi on their own initiative otherwise. "Would you believe my car was sandaled at Mount Scopus?"

"It still stings when you're shot wearing a vest," countered Aram. "Muzzle into your chest, those exploding blood packs."

"You're welcome," injected woozy Maliya.

"You've been declared dead and Ofer's trying to find a corpse with your likeness."

"What?" Maliya was hallucinating overhearing Ofer's name.

"I'd keep running if I were you," updated Ben.

"I knew it was something!" spouted Mussah excitedly. He was in the throes of whisking them for a try at Hadassah Ein Kerem when the intrigue started to make sense and his intermittent viewings of the Prime Minister by way of rearview mirror interchanged of course with regulation observations of the road caused him to offer up a sincerely gleeful "Welcome back!". "Tell me it wasn't an Arab," he continued, suddenly worried, hand on heart.

"Disgruntled relative," Aram tendered up front.

"Ohhh," Maliya groaned, bowing her head, twisting away from him in guilty anguish.

"Thank G-d." Mussah raised his focus and open palm skyward. The lone taxi endeavored to remain on the mountainside asphalt as Ben revised arrangements by cell, headlamps peering for less hostile neighborhoods. On the outskirts, these would be the ones, undisturbed by midtown cuffuffle, silenced on the verge of desert.

Grenade scavenged the morgue.

"Ofer has to impress Yuli," Ben hypothesized, weighing their case at present. "At any rate, you'll be superfluous," the cab rolling on cobblestones, halting a rock's throw from an empty landing bed.

Chapter Ten

The cabbie watched a giant brown-green copter fall into them from the heavens.

"Army?" the Prime Minister quipped.

"A guy I trust. He's on exercises."

Mussah lifted his eyebrows.

Ben corrected, "Practice."

"Thank G-d."

"Yes. He has air clearance and relative autonomy, in spurts. Flight control has to give us permission to occupy Israeli air space or we'll get brought down...a heap of debris."

"Oh my G..."

"Mussah," interrupting him. "Thank-you for your services. You are officially back on duty. Have you thought of an alibi for all this?" Ben asked rhetorically.

"My car was stolen," he declared triumphantly.

"Ah, that will require a police report which somebody will find. And then they will find you."

"Oh."

"Try this. You refill the missing gas, drive to a good walk from home, but close enough, and puncture a tire because you got a flat on Saturday night, your "big moneymaker. It made you so disappointed that you angrily ripped out the radio..."

"You tore apart the man's radio?"

"...not bearing to listen to the incoming calls from dispatch for those many lost customers. Garages aren't open tonight, giving you a larger time span than this specific interval. Spend your cash on utilities. Don't put it in the bank."

The instructions were logical, Mussah agreed. Aram and Maliya exchanged dubious looks. Not even a dirty seat. Ben had put the Prime Minister on a luggage tarp. As if they had never been there with him that night. They rose in that clamorous contraption which whipped a sandy draft upon the driver of a taxi. And were gone. Pleased with himself was he for helping save the Prime Minister of Israel. But he couldn't brag about it had it not been top secret, for so many reasons.

A whirlybird ride at low altitude navigating with headlamps in the eve. The pilot trailed landmarks on ground level, pitching steeply the craft at high speed as he did so. At least they couldn't hear Ben coaching from his play book over the rotor din. And they refrained from using the microphone headset so as to maintain strict radio silence, save tower communications. Maliya had their passports. Ben, an extra pair, just to be safe. Not chancing being stopped in a vehicle, by sky route the group would touch down at the strip. It was also quick. Convoluted methods although messier to arrange and offering more opportunities to get caught made for more pieces for antagonists to figure out and jigsaw together into a homogeneous whole than a straight line from A to B.

Advent at Atarot. The trio tripped over themselves clumsily dismounting from their winged chariot. They clunkered to a small plane on the tarmac. "Charter," expounded the aide displaying his brilliance. Not so easily explained to the customs contingent was the reservation with a pseudonym instead of the name of the dead Prime Minister of their nation. He was cleared. Time for Ben to relay a final anecdote. "Our airborne friend of moments ago was on coordinated movements in Nowhereville, Judah with a tank when I reconfirmed his RSVP by cell. Tankie was left making do by his lonesome, pretending to superiors all was well, when the bird took off with the big torch for a spell. We just fit into his bracket, we hope. Anyway, the ground roving buddy owed our man from, and this is whence came our epiphany, the event in which he drove his tank through the city streets..."

"I heard about that," confirmed Maliya.

"...to his parents' house, before the brothers and neighborhood friends who hadn't believed he was a tankist."

"And the pilot testified on his behalf at the court-martial?" smart-mouthed Aram.

"Our pilot got his slow-witted friend absolved."

"Then we're leaving you in good company." Aram rapped Ben on the shoulder.

"Which one?" gibed Maliya.

"I'm not betting on you," Ben shot back. "You're running on empty."

Anew they were on the move. Maliya was groggy in flight from her red cell donation and the day's adventures, spouting lectures of kabbalah and letter-counting. "Aram, two hundred and forty-one in gematria, rearranged to marah meaning to soar. Hidden is the bitterness, rebellion, exchanging the quiescent final letter a with h. Maliya, one hundred fifty-five, equalling kanah, acquired, equalling kaneh, a conduit shaft being the means to acquire. Ben, son of, also known by fifty-two which is brother-in-law yavam, director of plays bayam, becol kelev kaval...in all a dog chained. Loyal."

Her hallucinatory rantings frighteningly accurate, Aram prodded her for accounts on others, people she'd never met. "Yuli."

"July. Day, also fifty-six as well as his sea, his reservoir. Halvayah is a funeral, an escorting, company. Haliviyah would be the wreath which is also an accompaniment. Calu, they were consumed, perished. Calu, they measured and comprehended. Go! Lechu!" She was adding the numerical values assigned to each Hebrew letter and recreating the words, keeping their sums equal.

"Tal, Gadi," Aram suggested, Maliya coming in and out as if in wakened sleep.

"Tal and Gadi together totals fifty-six, lumping them in with Yuli and her commentary. Tal is short of being a mother. Tal plus a father gives mother."

Now, Aram had no occasion in which to reveal Maliya's parentage, hoping to shield her at present, as long as possible. He wasn't sure whether he'd tell her at all. There was great conflict. To destroy her life as she had known it. To destroy them as a couple. He deserved her. She deserved remain carefree. But she was in a place between reality and the spirits high in their plane, and she was in open communication with ...something. Some thing not holding back.

"Ofer. Ofer. They were different. They learnt. They hated." In the brief statements rallied between the gents in the taxi Maliya had realized her uncle's involvement in the assassination, again without Aram's entering into minute details for lack of proper pause in the happenings. "Shanu. Sanu. Three hundred and fifty-six, less than Aram and Maliya combined, who roamed, who swerved. Shatu. Satu. Hashai. A gift." She searched for him in his eyes.

And at that instant he vowed to not open the secret. Their plane listed sharply in a severe turn. Alarmed, Aram questioned the cockpit occupant.

"We've just been grounded," the pilot retorted. "Israel has hailed us to return immediately."

"Where are we exactly?" Aram demanded.

"Beyond the country's borders to be precise, including her water territory."

"Then they have no legal premise for a recall. You as pilot are the current authority of craft and crew safety in international airspace. Take us to Italy as per the approved flight plan."

"By violating domestic orders from flight control I risk incrimination."

"You're wrong. Change our course back to the original before we do reenter homeland executive jurisdiction and are subjugated to it."

Yuli watched the assassination videotape on

television when it aired, Ben's quote regarding the body resounding in her mind. Isn't that convenient, a camera on the shooting? The oddity of it was that instead of filming the goings on on stage where the stars were performing and the Prime Minister was in attendance, the photographer shot the gunman loitering around the limousine waiting area when there was nothing to see. Why was security allowing this guy to hang around a restricted zone anyway? And who was the cameraman? Reports said he was anonymous. What was all the talk of the whole thing being a fake? It looked like a setup. But was it real? Under normal circumstances a staged event is a mirage. Ben was erratic that night. All was not well. He darted off. Had it been hopeless he would have remained by her side. Something was astir.

On duty medical personnel the night in question also had their share of problems. Besides the requisite hospital and police statements to be made, illogical arrests were taking place. The subjects remanded into custody were none other than the children of the surgeons responsible for the Prime Minister's care. Nurses, technicians, extra workers on site, threatened. As witness they were rendered mum, person by person down the roster. Snagging the doctors' children, even for a short-lived cell visit, was a message. They could be gotten. Charged with bogus infractions, the cases obviously lacked legs, but the kids were seized by another's hand. It could be worse. Successful were the scare tactics.

The gunman gave up his university student friends as fellows in the ring. Trials were underway consisting of the lowest rungs on the ladder, all below age twenty-five. Not justice. A circus. These kids in court before the judge were laughing at the ridiculous nature of their charges...which stuck. The assailant had boasted of previous attempts on the Prime Minister, whether real or fabricated, and his audience had been legally obligated to advise the authorities of the threat he posed, which they did not.

Out of those files came their association in the radical religious group where discussions of a spiritual bounty on the Prime Minister for destroying the country were a mainstay. By this it was meant that they literally openly prayed for his death. So it was the religious sector of the nation which was responsible. The secular half cast upon them the blame. Ashamed, the right wing lay low. Only after several bus bombings occurred within days of each other and the people were afraid and sickened did the anti-peace movement regain momentum. Right and Left went head to head.

Ben was interviewed on air and expressed how he wasn't there the night his friend needed him most because of the car accident of his brother which took him clear across town. Seen once, his testimonial was then censored and not shown again. This relayed to Yuli its importance. Schemers had need of removing Aram's aide so he could not help him. That was not a lift to her emotional weight.

Then it started. Bodies flung without remorse. And their ranking in the coverage? Unjustifiably relegated to a mere post script as though they did not indicate culprits other than the one already behind bars. The Prime Minister's police guard. Suicide. Having survived Grenade's onslaught and recovered from his bullet, the fighter who had disguised himself in hospital garb and battled until exhaustion to set Aram free apparently could not overcome his profound sadness and sentiments of guilt at the PM's passing and so of his own volition just gave up. A high profile police officer. Suicide. What was his angle? He wasn't responsible for protecting Aram from up close. But he was engrossed enough in the fact-finding to note the blatant incongruities. Perhaps these bothered him...or others. And the inherent problem with suicide is that one doesn't merely instantaneously cease to be because one tires of breathing. It is a violent, painful, and physically difficult act to undertake, all these increasing in intensity as the act progresses. It requires planning and often superhuman strength to continue at the onset of the body's weakening. Factually, some suicides are impossible. For example, shooting yourself in the chest multiple times. Or, killing yourself a number of varying ways, simultaneously. These would demand outside assistance.

Fear not. Ofer walked. Reporters connected him socially and monetarily with the gunman. No legal reprisal. His official Shabak name was Grenade, organizer and leader of the charged student rebels, on film. Still a free man. He was placed handing the gun and bullets to his protégé assassin the day of the concert. Nothing.

Chapter Eleven

Times were dangerous. Yuli had her doubts
but refrained from pressing the point with Ben, who
offered cryptic sentences of encouragement as they
played the bereaved relations. Maybe it was best they
had no direct line to the niece. She was safer on her
own. That said, considering the revealing news stories
the public stayed largely complacent and gullible,
unable to fathom the scope of the secret service
conspiracy. Whoever bought the tale or kept mute
earned a spot among the living. The plain clothes
police escort knew nothing of the Prime Minister's
survival. He passed Grenade's test. Mussah? Lied lied
lied that flat tire gig. Not certain is it whether Grenade
entirely ruled him out or if the agent solely was
satisfied by Mussah's desperate will to propagate the
yarn. Believe, be quiet, or beguile. The Arab taxicab
driver added a method to the list.

There was further complication. Ben couldn't
quite locate Aram and Maliya. They were supposed
to hit untraceable preordained check-ins in Italy on
the way to a vacation stay on the coast. Thrashing
waters were the pair's inclination. Who knew why?
Alas, none were touched, and Ben knew this having

travelled the route personally. To specify, the
untraceable nature precluded anyone from receiving
word while in Israel, including the aide. Aram was to
retrieve locally originating planted mail from private
post boxes falsely named. He was to cash out blankly
addressed reimbursement cheques from Italian
furniture shops, to name a business, where Ben had
returned items previously purchased. Aram had left
no sign.

Beach life definitely agreed with the pair.
Maliya was as she was and Aram disguised himself in
facial scruff to be cautious. In empty parts they
resided and loafed, fellow residents not at all updated
in world affairs that be the couple's particular
business. Funny how a stretch of space travels one to
another realm. It needn't be a great expanse. Not able
to contact Ben or Yuli without reprisal, they hunkered
down and saw it pass. Madness. Well, there, in the
world of Ben and Yuli. Maliya and Aram's patch
breathed sunsets and aqua. Crimson, sky blue. Fire,
untamed pools. They lost their lives of earlier and in
so doing bathed in gratitude for having gained so
much. Hard to elaborate on, though akin to finding the
simple core beneath clothing riches. The garb a
softening comfort, yet they were ready.

He told her. Of her uncle as limousine
assassin. He told her. Of her adoption and faked
papers. He told her. Of the theory she was his niece
stolen. By the time that rolled around she practically
guessed he was going there. However, they had no
evidence Ofer was Seed. The two operations may be
parallel, never transecting. Aram was disturbed by the
timing, crossing through him and Maliya when he
interfered in the jail terms. Those three items, the
couple and their behaviour both individual and in
consort, collided with the physicist action. When the
Shabak is involved there are no coincidences. Where
did that put them? It was up to Maliya. Aram would
not turn from her again. Not was it in her mind to
desist from their love, but she was not who she was,
on paper. Why did paper impact so? The parchment
revealed lies unspoken. Without permission she had
been toyed with. Now she was aware, and had the
power.

Ben had the flight logs and was reading them
like a mystery novel. "...grounded..." No. "...beyond
air territory..." Good. "...radioed to come back..." Say
they didn't. Say they didn't. "...they did..." He
located their pilot to confirm the passengers'
whereabouts at last sighting.

"Yeah, I responded to the call to return to Israel."

Ben decided his answer was elusively vague. "You returned to Atarot."

"Correct."

"What happened to my friends? Do you remember it was me there that night? Did they land in Jerusalem with you?"

The pilot did recognize Ben. "I had to ascertain you were you, sorry."

"That's okay. I'm so many things," Ben joked. "I'm thankful you're protecting them."

"We made an unscheduled stop, unlogged. I'll lose my flying privileges."

"No no. I'm zipped. Repeat not."

"Eilat. That's where they touched down. Tropical paradise."

"Indeed. Good man. Great man!" he issued in celebratory style to the pilot's moral integrity, but mostly to himself. Ben was pumped, sassed, and looking for a vacation.

On the five hour drive south in a rented car, surmising his own transmitted a signal as to its whereabouts, Ben was touring within the synapses. The western shore, outskirts of town. How tough could it be? Not optimal was it that the late Prime

Minister was still a resident of Israel, though. Had
they only made it to Europe. Or, was it an idea to
resurface? Publicity of not dying would be life
support. Then questions would eventually indicate
Grenade who would be desperate enough to tamper
with Aram's car. Bad plan. New identities. Aram and
Maliya were ahead of him. Whoa. Now he fathomed
the argument for not driving down this road. That's
where the bus toppled over the side last month.
Maniac! That truck was over the line. Didn't rental
companies install positioning devices as well, to curb
thefts? The technology at a reasonable price may not
have reached here, yet. Map it on foot. Allow a few
days.

"Ben!" Holidaying Maliya in a large foreign
sun hat spied him in her viewfinder poking the area. "I
have a waterproof bag for subsurface shots," she
answered in reply to his questioning face.

"Aram?"

"Of course. He bought it saying it deserved
me, at which point I whined 'Aw, what did it do?'
sympathetically. That videotaped shooting gave us
the idea."

"Out of the ashes..."

"So?"

"Patience, madame."

"Ben," shouted Aram mezzo forte when Maliya brought him home. "Long enough," he criticized. "So?"

"You too? No 'We're glad you survived the journey, friend.', 'How did you ever find us, you genius?', 'Where are you staying?', 'Are you hungry?', 'Thirsty?', 'What can we do for you?'"

"Go ahead." He faced Maliya, "This will only take a minute."

"Thank-you so much. It was tough, but well... In a small rental vehicle. Yes. Yes. Invite me to stay while I'm in town."

"Alright. But the last one, you don't blend, and you drew a bee line here."

"Yanking. I wanted it to hurt. Anyway, the test. DNA says you two are not related. Resume the good stuff at once."

They were struck. Aram misplaced his niece once more. Maliya, her entire genetic heritage. As for the second part, thanks for the sentiment but they were anyway. And that piece at least would be clearer now.

"It fit together nicely. Well..."

Aram protested, "It doesn't make sense like this."

"Not everything is an evil trick, Aram. Some

"things just occur randomly, falling where they will on whom they will. Our finding each other may not be the catastrophic catalyst for the horrific killings of your family. I might just be illegally adopted, unrelated to you, and we met. My uncle's undertakings could be work, politically motivated, disconnected from our relationship. We cannot know everything. Next you'll be asking why life exists, what your purpose is in the grand scheme. You want too much. You may not get it. I don't wish you torture yourself. Let it flow."

Recalling how she'd allocated their roles with uncanny precision via gematria while asleep nonetheless, Aram presented Maliya with a lengthened glare.

She gestured back a lack of comprehension.

Ben broke the emoting with fact. "You must leave."

"Should I walk into Egypt declaring myself the late and very Jewish Prime Minister of Israel as Islamic radicals make me true to my word? A never-ending boat ride around the third world? I can't cross the border to Jordan and I made peace with them."

"Try an encore of the plane thing. Traffic is moving. I'll set you up. Your optimism is refreshingly familiar, remember I buried you."

"I saw. Who was that?"

Ben shrugged. "Although it was an excellent turnout. The bitter ex-wife and her new husband were faucets. Every despot who was any despot attended."

"How is Yuli?"

"Watching out for her. Extremely perceptive, begging the heavens for a merciful outcome."

"Inform my sister-in-law," Aram charged.

"Always my intention," corrected Ben, "once you've emigrated. She's already on our wavelength."

As the conversation flipped to mystical, Aram wide-angled on his two partners of sorts, picturing Yuli, all of them a bit off. There was nothing to add. Nevertheless, he began...No. Leave it alone.

They had slipped into nonchalance as days flashed by lacking peril. Grenade had been shadowing the aide. He too was in Eilat slinking around the premises, and his reconnaissance managed to update him on Maliya's newfound hatred for her pseudo-family, especially one uncle. A crucial development. To kill Aram and force a reunion? Toughie Maliya would sooner bury Ofer with her bare hands, and a side order of the criminal parents. Their family was destroyed. She had come from bad stock. Take them both out? He practically raised her. Stole her in the

first place due to her loveliness. Angelic. Many
options. The goal as usual, to solve the dilemma in the
long term.

Ofer allowed them board and depart. Not so
much benevolence as the easiest and most beneficial
outcome. Maliya desired the man Ofer was destined
to destroy, the bloodletting would be nonexistent, and
Ofer's sister should not encounter her daughter's
present attitude. Such was their will to escape,
incognito, it required no effort from Ofer to close the
case. Besides, it was not that he hated Aram per se,
but that Aram's elimination one way or another was
in his best interest. He could not hurt Maliya, he was
pretty sure. They were willing participants in the
concealment of his crimes, including preserving what
remained of family life in Dan region, so a few lies
later there need be no messy cleanup. The best
business solution was laid in his hands: do nothing.
He was professional evil, sure. And they had been
tremendous foes, all, as amply demonstrated. She was
theirs. He watched his niece go.

Chapter Twelve

Aram and Maliya hopped countries in planes of many sizes until they got to Hawaii. After they had loosened the tension of Israel and the intrigue therein life developed into a different routine, Aram trumpeting a series of social causes with his legal training, Maliya arting in a variety of media. The climate lent itself to renewable energy technology which they installed as a tribute to Gadi and Tal and the myriad of sabra solar hot water heaters dotting all the roofs of the condos of their homeland. "Why don't they do this where we come from?" raised Maliya as they kinked necks skyward toward whooshing wind turbine blades which fed their house with alternating current.

"Beautiful."

"Do you travel back in your dreams, Aram, to say 'hi'?"

"Only in nightmares." He grinned teasingly.

"Cranky exile."

"They did us a favour."

"Life takes you where you'll go...kicking and screaming."

"Fate and master plan?" humoring her.

"I don't know why anything is anything. I

"only know what I like." Maliya beamed at him with a devilish glow.

"I can work with that." Catching her wavelength, Aram intimated readiness to embrace her by nearing when she jokered about, taunting him into a chase. They had a small place on the water. Palms sprung naturally from below and loomed far above them to offer specks of shade. Still trapped by oceans or seas. Things change. And remain the same.

In Jerusalem, Ben trotted the narrow concrete passages leading to Yuli's apartment and an expectedly upbeat visit. Photo in hand, he gleefully burst from the door frame area into her salon, fanning the atmosphere and baiting her to grab it to receive the news. She took the photograph and froze, her legs quivery, her lips numb. What was this? Swallowing, eyes tearing. Ben went for the image but it was snared in the trap of Yuli's steeled fingers and he could not pry it loose.

"Yuli, it's me here on the left, in Eilat. I'm wearing the same shirt," Ben tried, pointing at the similarities, grabbing at his fabric. She did not understand the shot was evidence everything was okay. He could bring her along, he thought.

She didn't hear. "Why would you do it?" she

yelped, bawling.

"The date, Yuli. It's two days ago. This is Aram, me, and...Maliya in Eilat two days ago."

"Aram?"

"He's alright."

"Aram." Her mind was landing on terra firma once more.

"He and Maliya flew to Hawaii to stay safe. They're there now."

"Aram survived. The assassination...it's what we both surmised, right, Ben? You confirmed it for me. Thank-you. I trusted you'd come through." She was monotoning her half of a sane dialogue without conviction, unnerving Ben in the process. A breakdown would've been more normal. He didn't get this pretense when it was a coup Aram was not murdered, especially considering his girlfriend's identity. Yuli was handling him, and herself, for looking into that picture she did not see Aram and Maliya although her intellect knew that it was. Ben was there, in the dated picture, looking like he was at present, even wearing the same clothes. It was Aram, she saw that. She wasn't completely off. But she also saw a younger Gadi and Tal in their place. And the more Yuli absorbed it the stronger the feeling. Goose bumps. Chills. This Maliya, this girl, she was Yuli's dead sister's double. Her smile and the manner in which she scrunched her face and kinked her head was Tal. As sisters they grew up only years apart. She could spot the resemblance of Tal's spawn to all the family, herself and her own mother included. Yuli mustered every bit to stay calm. She couldn't. Wishing Ben wasn't there, she was overwrought. Before Yuli realized what she was saying she heard her voice shout out loudly in a tone she couldn't recognize as her own, "Aram's found our niece!" and listened to the declaration as if hearing it from someone else and for the first time and got a start. Fretting about appearances, he would think her mad now.

Rather, Aram's buddy greeted the proclamation with characteristic enthusiasm which Yuli would have anticipated had she been privy to the bulk of his private dealings. "I had reached the same conclusion. You'd never guess where she's been. But the DNA test I ran didn't match."

He was validating her without question, save lab results contradicting the entire theory. Unheard of, this improbable credit. "DNA test?" she parroted.

"Negative," he repeated.

She sensed his disappointment in the finding and followed suit in her own feelings. Then she got it, a ray. "Who did you sample?" she probed with renewed courage.

Ben's lights were flickering in order to reach full glow. A blur yet, but he was receiving a transmission from her, not sure what. "Maliya against Aram." Could that be it?

"Not me!" Yuli was ecstatic. Of course she could pick out her own niece. She just knew who she was. Just like that. Obviously, he hadn't known. He didn't know.

Bulb at maximum intensity. Some hurried figuring. His face transformed to portray the glee. Ben was there, too, in all out celebration.

Through intermediary Ben, Yuli was notified. Having spent the majority of her years investigating into the truth, she was due. And so in the photo she was presented with the puzzle's last piece. The moment brought her quiet heart. However, for all her effort and angst, perhaps wasted years trying unravel others' knots in the bindings they tied around everyone else, it was the man who seemingly continued forward in his self-directed pursuits who stumbled upon the prize. Fluke? Or was even his path to great success divinely guided for such a purpose? Aram brought Maliya close with his desire, but he kept her in defiance of suspicion, trials and

disappointment with a ceaselessly indentured soul
that loved. He, an active participant in earthly living,
reaped the fruits for which he labored, but not the
knowledge. Or was that another blessing? Yuli, all in
her head, shunning her own existence because of the
pain. It was her. She got the word, a product of
patient waiting and occasional plea.

"Maliya." Yuli savored the name and imbibed
her visage. Tal was alive in this girl.

"What was her former identity?" Ben inquired.

She was ready to say it when her throat
seized. "There's no point."

He was surprised, but he was fresh in the
maze. For her, defeat had long been conceded to
reality.

"Maliya is prettier than the first one," blurted
Yuli playfully. "What's she like?"

Ben was impressed by Yuli's transformation.
In a span of minutes she had regressed twenty to
thirty years, and it had been necessary. The fifteen
year old kid returned to cavort with her twenty year
old sister, the one in the picture, not like she was a
wizened and troubled aunt at all. "Fairly easy-going,
in light of, well...She and Aram are in love." He
broached this subject tenderly, unsure of consequent
reactions.

"Aram?" Obviously. They were together living in Hawaii. Until Ben said it aloud it hadn't clicked.

Ben awaited her response, in tension.

Yuli was misted in ambiguity. Then emerged her figure into the clear. "The kids are living." She was doting aunt again, pleased with their fortune, inspired by their positive endurance, pledging to learn from their example.

Amazing. The lost niece had been invisible to Aram and Ben and his barrage of tests, standing right in front of them all the while, but for this woman it took only one look at a photo to confirm. Once done, nothing could convince her otherwise. It would have taken a single pass by in the streets of Jerusalem...But that never occurred.

"Maliya's not scarred?"

"Reads her past like a book. No recollection."

"Good," assented Yuli, internally referring to her new enjoyment policy.

Ben extended his hand to shake with hers, grasping the concept via diffusion. "Great," piercing her with his grin.

She laughed as her smile broke free.

The sound echoed over Hawaii and two

shadows splashing knee-deep to the sunset, nary a care about dinner. Inside, ruffling the edges of the pages was their breeze having a go at her writing abandoned on the table, weighted under a rock:

His eyes are still soft for me
body wanting more
searching hands grasping out mute words
darkness breathes of him
a wave envelopes me
turn 'round he's there.

His skin sweet of light sleep
inhale him close
a glance twisting caught on me
stunned winded anew
his grip finds my arm
I didn't know he'd stole near
his eyes are still soft for me
we cease to touch.

Bracing a secret
one that binds me hunts him
stares straddling the room
his blue eyes ride me green.

In a dream
I am walking out on the grassy pier
wetter and wetter it becomes beneath bare feet
approaching the edge
the water has risen up to my knees in the reeds
the scene flips
and finds me launched into the waters' expanse
sitting on a pod of sticks bound with twine
wading out, wading, there is my boat
it comes at me fast
and strikes the pod underneath
but the boat when in view is a coffin black
I lift the lid, bail and embark waving the shore
paddling off into the endless sea.

I ask why I'm here and dream
there is gunfire on Har HaTzofim
a past time preceding schools, before outposts
Yerushalayim erupts in explosions
I take to the tunnels under the hill
maneuvering through the maze
knowing the way
guiding a child from battle
we again escape underground
then I am blind
light shooting from my eyes

yet somehow I still am
able to traverse the subterranean paths.

My hand clutches a purple ticket
tilting it as a rudder in flight over Akko
I rise to the height of an escarpment
with a brightly lit city below
and land at a hotel
requesting to rest in the daughters' bed
so as not to lose my flying pass.

There is a pool inside the ocean
past lovers drowning under wave comforters,
caught inside the cotton
and there are couples who can breathe
under waves as duvets
guiding me with a light
he takes me through the waters.

Lying choking in bed
I see the light and want to it
an awesome bird stands in between
charcoal feathers of unearthly power
my mother calls at me from the door
near sleep she awoke with a terrible sensation.

His fingertips tingle my face
whisp'ring strands of hair to the east
palms introduce
lips stroking my neck
it desires them and they are eager.

His tongue spears the blackness with sound
slides through my spine
mouths groping
kisses embracing
wandering smooth limbs
and they are eager
and they are eager.

by Maliya

Chapter Thirteen

Her shade of blonde in the sun paraded itself golden copper. For all their practice that year it was a wonder there had not been a pregnancy by her handsome love. Stress, possibly. After all, it was a hectic time. The army, university, his dangerous work. And that explosive night when he was next to death. Had his partner not yanked him out of the trouble, she wouldn't have a husband at all. It did not seem long since the tropical wedding, but no reportable baby activity. And they wanted there to be, so the couple deferred to professionals as intellectuals tend to do, experts capable of yielding results under any condition. Whatever it took. For, although they were no longer in the country of their parents and heritage there remained still a suffocating social pressure to breed their genes onward. She kept the remnants of her clan apprised of the happenings, but he was more secretive. Males and their Middle Eastern pride, and so forth, his reticence was understandable in regard to relaying the goings on about his goings off. And the culture's attitude on the subject of meddling with nature and biology. They'd be creating obstacles for their child to overcome in society in the ensuing decades. How responsible is that? But they melded into each other. That was all the truth they needed. Love walks its own path.

"Yuli's waiting for me," she halfheartedly pleaded as her husband wrapped around her shoulders his comfortingly reassuring arms. "I can't wait to spend this time together. We'll have a lot of fun, us girls."

"She was great making the arrangements," he added, already melancholic he wasn't travelling too. It wasn't possible under the circumstances.

"I know it seems like a long trip," she consoled, herself as well as him, when he decided to interrupt the motions of her lips with his own. The train of thought gone, nothing left to do but join in. There it was, mid-kiss. She remembered the reasoning behind their separate vacation. "And I'm not returning until I've got our baby."

"Whatever the case may be."

"What it shall be." They embarked on additional oral mining expeditions, mouths not wishing let go. No more of the other variety of pleasuring at this late moment. Enough of that already. Never enough. "You, be careful."

Bored with her sweet obstinate concern, "Wife," he dismissed her in as mannerly a fashion as he could so as to disguise his dismissiveness.

It didn't work. She hadn't just fallen out of the persimmon tree. "Husband," she sent back in like mode.

He nodded in acknowledgment of her willingness to engage.

"I'm worried about your politicking. My colleagues have expressed concern. They say you're playing a dangerous game. Our country isn't above taking out people making waves. Remember that story about Lechi killing the Israeli girl because she was in love with an Arab?"

"Tal."

"No, I want my husband."

"What sort of a husband am I who can't father his own family? It's what they did to me. And it's a job. I'm an expert, like my associates where I work, and we're being subjected to outrageous radioactive conditions in our employment environment. They're killing us, Tal, with cancers and sterility. You can't ask me not to be angered."

"Come to the university with me, Gadi."

"They won't listen to outsiders. I have to maintain access to meet with top security personnel on the boards. Once I'm out I'm out. I will also have an obligation to silence. As it is, I am merely trying to help myself and fellow workers, not hurt the nuclear "industry. I'm not doing anything wrong. My intentions are for the Israeli people. Anyone can see that."

"We will have our family. Don't jeopardize that."

"I have a right. I know what I'm doing."

"My little sister's waiting, Love," changing the tone of their discourse.

She softened him. "Let's not fight, Tal. You're leaving."

"At least you won't have to suffer my hormonal fluctuations and mood swings from the drugs. Yuli's opted to bear those with me."

"Brave girl."

"Unsuspecting."

He took her hand. "Not too much talk of this back in our country, please."

"When I give birth and register the baby, you're still the legal father."

"That's not enough, Tal. You know I have to be the father, period. We can't have them casting aspersions on your child. We have to protect it."

"Religion doesn't influence me, Gadi."

"It's not about us. A person can't go to the Rabbinate and freely marry if he doesn't know who his parents are. That's not fair to impose upon an "innocent child, if we can change the facts."

"He or she will fly off to Europe to wed. We'll raise him or her to be independent."

"Foreign medical records will never reach here. This was always the plan."

"So you won't confide in your family?"

"Our situations differ immensely. It will be your baby. There's nothing to be ashamed of."

"Neither should you be."

"Never." This breathy word followed by his slow savoring lips entangled with hers softly barely touching, and the squeeze of hands holding fabric vestment containing no body, a light brush of his fingers on her cheek, were their good-bye.

And summer snow melts
to find the lost bud blossomed
there in my garden.

Garreted in newsprint was Green Eyes, receiving Yuli's tiding, fronting emotionlessness. He sat, and he sat, in all much longer than he had intended.

Outside that small room, around the corner, a few floors above, Ofer was also on break in the national headquarters. His surly state complementary to the man by some stories separated, engulfed in the paper. In need of inventing a tale for the parents to explain her disappearance and lack of communication, something uplifting. She eloped and sent her regards. That would do. He could omit the whole loathing part, et cetera. With this accomplished he shovelled in the tachina-drenched chips on his shawarma. A day's pay. Not bad.

Flash back to the couple and their copper-head baby, Yuli vicariously mothering this child whose traits receded through the women of Tal's heritage. They all draped her with attention as she was quite the achievement. Gadi's younger brother, who could have been his own son, even paused from his teenage wildness long enough to notice the cutie lump. "Look. She loves him," the sisters teased, consciously eroding his cool factor. Aram returned the favour and handed her over when she smelt.

Flash to the parents of their copper-head child whose traits receded through the women of Tal's heritage. They furiously moved overnight as instructed, signed forged documents wherever Ofer pointed to make false claim to the authorities, terrified of getting caught. "You are our child, our lovely Maliya," the pair would repeat, "and it is embedded in our minds and hearts the moment to us you were born." They centred their lives on the coast, shunning Jerusalem. They extinguished the life she had had for two years before they'd forcefully claimed her. They all draped her with attention as she had been quite the achievement.

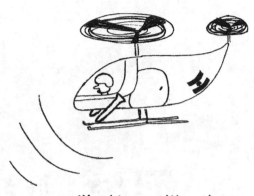

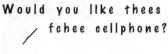
Would you like thees
fchee cellphone?

...Eet eez
fohr you.

Uh, no thanks.

The Draft

The Draft

book 2

Chapter One

"You are not going to Israel!" her mother
screamed. Unfortunately, this didn't quite ring with
the effervescence of the "Get out of my house!" she'd
been reciting the months before.

"What are you going to do, lock me in my
room for the rest of my life?"

A pause. She was actually considering the
particulars of that room thing.

And there it was, the pilot already having
begun their descent while still over the Mediterranean
lest they wound up brunching with King Hussein.
And the twelve hour flight had only taken five days,
the scenic route via Romania at the hands of an
unscrupulous travel agent whose last words were to
the tune of "Once you get to Bucharest I think you
will want to stay a while...to visit."

"Welcome to the balagan," greeted the security
despot trying to be nice. The voyage didn't make
sense, really. She felt to be on the receiving end of
some spiritual homing device to a place she'd never
been, a Hebraic signal sent to a non-Jewish Scot.

Surprisingly there were others like her.
"There's this book, see," an exasperated exchange

student piped off to one very confused Israeli customs inquisitor as the girl fumbled through her luggage to pluck out Exodus by Leon Uris. As an answer to "What are you doing in the country?", One Year Program at Hebrew U. would have also sufficed. Then again, this made for better storytelling for the American girls on the cots of the infamous Thousand dormitory - built hurriedly in the style of army barracks on Exalted Hill during one siege or another in Jerusalem - somewhere between "My boyfriend gave me crabs...but he's a construction worker" and "Never have your genital warts lacerated at a teaching hospital...even if you save money."

Security-wise no one could make up their minds. The Canadians tested every item electronic or electric in nature to assure themselves it worked only in the manner for which it was intended, whilst the Communists removed all batteries so that nothing would work at all. The Israelis were unseasonably lax as the luggage had all been previously combed through by the Communists, though their bathroom stall-checking remained supreme and via personal interface and subjective intuitive judgement they can always see through you anyway, when the Americans who had gasped upon viewing the electronics bag under x-ray didn't bother to even open it. But the Germans, thinking that if they analysed the particle residue opaquely covering her synthesizer they'd hit the mother load of homemade explosives manufacturing, were dismayed to find an ordinary young woman and evidence of an obscenely dusty house.

An Israeli bus ride is unlike any other, each driver playing exotic music of his choice, careening around edges of mountains at illegal speeds as the floor noticeably lists to aid in the turn, one or two shattered windows held together only by the plastic coating on either side. Unless of course the crazy post-army operator raced past your stop or if it was Shabbat, in which event you'd need to walk. From right to left a sign reminds its passengers "not to spit, throw, or crack open seeds" as its newcomer gently nudges the shaft of the neighboring M-16 off of direct line of fire to her foot. "Forgiveness soldier, perhaps to move your weapon? I descend here." It was... emptiness. The driver pointed at her to make a right.

Soon from that direction appeared the kibbutz van. Without a verbal exchange proving necessary, or for that matter possible, the respective blue, black, and red giant hockey bags were loaded in displacing in their midst a sizeable group of native kibbutz students to the side of the road alongside the new volunteer.

Foreign Hebrew-student laborers on the Israeli

cooperative settlements were as diverse as they come.
There was a small-man who was relieved of
greenhouse duty after one too many tomato vines had
unintentionally become dwarfed before its time during
twining. An unsettling phenomenon surfaced
concerning the super strong local tomato clip knockoff
which clamped onto that vine cutting and strangling it
unlike the European original which was designed for
weakness so as to release or tear as the plant grew.
Job opportunities included but were not limited to
plant stimulation with a vibrating wand - we should
all be so lucky - if you could live with blackened
hands, collecting hot dishes and cutlery from a moving
triangular industrial washing machine which should
conjure up episodes of Lucy on the assembly line...
plus heat, fruit picking: not as fun as it sounds, and
vegetable preparation while stomping on scorpions
from the crates.

So Swedish volunteers performed midnight
commando halva raids on the kitchen, Mexicans
mimed illicit impromptu finger shows which often
required explanations. Field wanderers, drinkers, the
art of bonfire. But Miami was a case. "Mum, mum,
thanks for the cheque. You see, the thing is that this is
a big farm and I haven't spent the last five thousand
dollars you sent me. Money doesn't even change

"hands at the local store." Needless to say he won the What Did Your Parents Bribe You With So You'll Go Home? competition, overshadowing the usual apartment and car with all of the above plus a yacht. In case you were wondering, the curious Toronto girl in question was later informed by her mother that they had considered a bribe but relented from actually offering one as that would have been an insult to her integrity. Extra points for creativity.

Would that have been the same integrity that joked to Bronx that the ulpan manager was heading to her room, provoking horrified yowling as she dropped her full mug of coffee to the ground and tore down the path guilt-ridden with visions of graffiti-covered white walls? Or the morality which as her friends so delicately phrased "averaged one man a month"? Then there was the time it took the kibbutzniks two hours to break her security code Tarom Airlines from inside their irrigation factory computerized programming so they could remove her name from the table of contents. Now, when he approached her in the dining hall calling her "criminal" she was genuinely relieved to find that was the reason and not that her secret cookie collecting expeditions had been discovered. Again, to what set of impossible standards can you hold an eighteen-year-old who has been known to buy at the house of pharmaceuticals fungicide and condoms in one fell swoop?

"Get down on the floor, down on the floor!" It was Miami causing mischief. "...Now speak Spanish to me."

And the kibbutzniks also had their quirks. The ulpan manager who within the first minutes of meeting you hands over a giant squeegee - "You'll need this." - created an outing as one of their mandatory monthly explorations of the country around collecting her new dog. Then again, on a subsequent religious kibbutz program a rather sadistic manager organized a visit to a chicken slaughterhouse and frequently probed whether Stick Out Like a White Girl In the Desert was a reporter. Thus, phone calls to her mum, in contrast to Miami's, ended with the repetitive plea to tape her mail. In light of this the "dog trip" as it came to be known didn't seem quite so bad. There was the tour guide who sent a certain hyperactive girl - who shall go unnamed - to circumvent the Caesaria amphitheater via the narrow cliff side with the heavily accented reasoning "It's good for you." After attempting to have her splattered over the rocky Mediterranean banks his second personality surfaced, that of private troubadour.

But London really did jump off the Ramon

crater declaring, "Good-bye cruel world," as twenty people ran to the edge to find him on a ledge a generous metre below the surface. "I said good-bye!" the English lad reiterated.

"Thanks for the nice, uh, central location" was the last thing Miami muttered as he and his mother raced out of the hired bus, dodging cars as they frantically clambered across the Tel Aviv highway where the driver had come to full stop right there in the middle of three roaring lanes to deposit them in plain view of the La Guardia exit ramp which they then ascended on foot.

Romance also featured into the day-trips: They found themselves together when the group fanned out onto the desert mountain. "I want to show you something beautiful." Armed Accompaniment held out his hand which she grasped. He led her off the path to the edge of a lone stream.

"That is beautiful," resounded the deep voice ...of Denmark who had followed along too.

Pitch black. Air raid sirens blare up and down. Jets overhead. Blasts of sound. Windows quiver noisily.

"Ayrden!"

"Yeah?"

"Someone wants you."

"Ayr, your machine gun boys are here."

"Okay, I'm coming. Tell them to wait." Life wasn't dull in yeshiva.

It hadn't been boring on kibbutz either - "Everyone duck! Ayrden's got the gun. Who keeps giving Ayrden the gun?" - but the rabbi wasn't ready for a religious student who received firearm lessons from neighborhood army patrols, who bought all her white chocolate from Armenians, who weren't Jewish...because they were Armenian, and who sat late at night in the booth with the Arab parking lot attendant to watch Thirtysomething.

It was the time of Desert Storm. The threats, the passionate hysteria...and that was just the parents of the girls in the academy. "Do you want to know what my feelings are?" Uh oh. The emotion awareness circle had come around to her with an ominous foreboding that this was not going to go well. The kabbalist who had been attempting to soothe frazzled nerves with mystically inspired guitar playing discreetly increased the volume. "My feelings are that I am sick of everyone talking about their feelings. Do your own internal calculations. If you sense you're in danger, run. I personally don't hear any alarms sounding," failing to mention the air raid siren she had taped and was playing over and over to scare the neighbours, "therefore it is my belief that nothing terrible is going to happen to me. But I can't speak for any of you."

Realistically considering the climatic temperament of the Jewish quarter of the old city of The G-d's Inheritance, They Will See Peace, or plain old Yerushalayim, for a missile to permeate the windy rainy atmosphere with any kind of biological or toxic gas, liquid, or solid component it would've had to land in the adjacent parking space. Falling on top of you wouldn't be so good either. That said, there didn't seem to be much reason for half the population of Tel Aviv to suddenly decide to visit their relatives in the capital or for the boys in the sister yeshiva to be concerned when their fellow prayers at the ancient temple's Western Wall panicked at the air raid siren and locked them out of the shelter. You would think the safest place in Israel would be beside the Dome of the Rock when under Arab attack. But when one's own government has its army dole out gas masks, skin powders, atropine injections, body suits, and perhaps escalate the effort to include large antibiotic doses, one sort of gets the message it is telling its people "War is at the door. Shhh." And in the crisis of sealed rooms, aluminium-covered water jars, you had to know somebody made a killing: scotch tape merchants, the phone company, and a perpetually sold out peanut butter puff junk food called Bamba.

Israelis certainly bear a unique perspective on combat practices such as offense as the best defense but you have to wonder who would give a semiautomatic weapon to a kid who passed the psychological the second time. Then there are the riflemen on kibbutzim in sensitive border areas who assemble on the rooftops in the event of enemy attack ...because extranational terrorists can't shoot vertically? In the end every action comes down to a probability of survival, like avoiding the middle of a bus where suicide bombers hang out.

What then was the chance your religious roommate in a harmless misguided personification would ask the bus driver if she could mount him? Perhaps the same as if she'd embrace watching others eat cookies on fast days - Ayrden - while she voluntarily passed out. Like the ex-boyfriend said, "You don't have to fast on Yom Kippur but you don't have to eat meat and cake either." He also said, "We'll empty and refill it and you'll pee again. So what'll we have accomplished by that?"

"I guess I didn't need to press the button," spilled the Westerner to his buddy as the entire accordion double-sized public transportation vehicle halted in the centre of town and completely emptied. Americans make interesting sport out of the Middle East as uncivilized civilization. "Great country it is," they boast, "if not for the locals." One day Ayrden's friend was venting on the subject of "their tight clothes, bad attitudes and dyed red hair" with which she was fed up as Ayr listened, nodding appreciably, attempting to remain inconspicuous in snug little shorts and t-shirt, her Hebridean head flaming all the while in the midday sun.

They get a kick out of the pirate radio station ship which supports Abie Natan who was jailed for meeting with Arafat prior to the later time when it became fashionable to shake the terrorist's hand and give him guns, pelf, and a slice of autonomy, opening its broadcast with "From somewhere in the Mediterranean...[gulls chirping]...we are The Voice of Peace." They find unfathomable the differences in policy of the left or right coalition governments. One gives away large chunks of territory, the other takes it back. With this in mind, when asked in job interviews back in the guerilla warfare zone of Toronto, Canada who or what party was currently in power the reply "Does it matter?" was often given and more often than that not well received.

There was Chief Justice Barak who invalidated legally valid laws at whim on the grounds they were not in the spirit of the principles on which their modern liberal democratic society was based. He did the same with laws which were not in the spirit of those principles on which the society should be based, if its people engaged in legal actions which were not becoming of an enlightened forward-looking nation, only, they didn't know it yet. In short he rewrote the law, but he did it with righteousness and flare.

But the delicious Mediterranean diet was not to be maligned, healthy and cheap because it's plant-based. "Animal, vegetable, mineral," a native recites gleefully pointing to a gold chain "chai" atop the chest hair foliage protruding from his open shirt before proceeding northward to his head.

Chapter Two

At eighteen Maliya had been mobilized to the
I.D.F. as were most citizens her age. Distinct from the
other high school draftees she was privileged to be
selected into the choice arts troupe, likely with the
assistance of familial protection. "Have you ever done
any acting?" the company inquired after the fact.

"People are always telling me I should. You
know, 'Act responsibly young lady', 'Would you
care to try acting like a human being, or at least as if
you give a damn?' But I don't want to be an actor. I'd
prefer to be my own character, the best me I can be."

"We think you've peaked," they deadpanned.

"I've been doing some composing about
radiation:

> Ode to the air
> You gave me cancer
> I loved you most of all
> Till I met with the B-cell enhancer
> ...Aaah!

And right enough she did repeatedly attempt to send
out her DVD, meeting with such responses as "This
is a radio station" and "I'll give you our fax number."

"It appears as though you produced the whole movie in your living room."

Exuberantly, "I burnt it myself."

"Student quality, a beginner painter incorporating all the colours."

"I didn't go to film school," she expelled with pride. Remarking on the frame where it was paused, "Looks like a skull, eh? That's my jacket."

Morose Writer rendered a dramatized section from his play Haze:

> The source of the pyre. Before I am
> able to inhale a last early gasp it chain-
> cuffs my ankles and squeezes them
> tight. The spigots clink clink clink-clink-
> clink reeling me in.

"Tribute to Edgar Allan Poe, the musical?" came the critique.

"It's a children's story."

"Give me some of that," motioned the comic in order to salvage their scanty material. "[Yeah,] I know of mind's dungeon. [Naw,] it's not difficult to arrive," he recited flippantly while miming directional hand gestures as if answering a tourist. "At the ominous spear-studded gates impeded from smooth "swing, across the crawling muck, by skull fragment pebbles and other bits of charred bone."

The group auditioning each other was silent, fixated on the incongruent representation.

"Well, it isn't!"

Eyes converged on the musician.

She ad-libbed in a Chinese accent, "Bahgain basement piano wessons. Leahning so intense they won't heah you scweam. An advertisement for Suzuki piano."

"What's with all the bleakness? This is the army."

"Let's go with the eccentric scientist thing."

"Is there any other kind?" A consensus was reached.

"Maliya, you can finally add that little c to the B.S. behind your name," another compressional wave sounded.

"So you'll help me?" she replied toward its origin.

Distracted, the girl beside her clarified, "This is usually the point where someone doubles over laughing."

Maliya began her pitch before they waived the concept altogether. "A physics lecturer rushes into class in a whirlwind to excitedly spout off an "unintelligible artsy allegory on the quantum number:

> <u>Come on n, you're going way too slow!</u>
> If you imagine yourself the perpetual
> traveller, only with the condition that
> you do it in a Concorde, you can get a
> great overview of the entire globe before
> the question arises about what you'd
> prefer for lunch. One blurry European
> country after another, even blurrier
> cities. How many was that? Ten or ten
> thousand? As long as the continents
> contain cities with working airports and
> planes capable of refuelling and
> transporting supplies while airborne,
> it's inconsequential. That's what's so
> classic about luxury travel.
>
> But wait! This dream is about to turn
> nightmare. The steward, rechecking
> passenger lists, discovers that your
> name...

"We need to stop and elect a name here,"
interjected the crowd taking proper character.

"I vote Ploni. Always liked that certain so and

"so."

"Anonymous nomination for Almoni."
"Shimon."
"Reuven."
"Those four are always causing trouble."
"Shlomo."
"Oh ho," approving.
"Shlo-mo, Shlo-mo," two chanted.
Maliya incited a show of hands for finality.
"Shlomo it is."

Cheers. "We knew you could do it, Shlomi."
"Very well.

The steward, rechecking passenger lists,
discovers that your name...Shlomo...was
dropped from the computer during a
slight power surge and saddling you
with parachute shoves you out the wing
door. Ah huh! That continuum of dot-
cities sending up Swanson's quickly
gains new meaning when you'd like to
land in one of them. Their distribution,
whether huddled densely along the
winding river of the plains or perched
one atop each lonely mountain peak,
strangely becomes pertinent when you

have to walk from one to the other
collecting spoons. So you traded
Beluga for blisters. It's all the same
stuff, just more extreme...Hey, look! Is
that your Concorde? Hey! Hey!

"And that is the layman's version of the
correspondence principle."

"Are you kidding?"

"A greater understanding will become
apparent through the Millikan oil drop experiment
'Yo Greaseball, get in like charge with e!' Lab reports
due next week. By this time you should also be caught
up with 'What the h is wrong with you 475
nanometres?'"

"Permission to be blue, sir?"

"Thanks to the Planck photoelectric effect. On
that note, uplifting renewable energy project 'Without
the sun we'd all be dead' Mr. Oulli, Bern. Next week
the adventures of the periodic table superheroes. Any
questions, corrections, comments?"

"This course is decreasing my will to live."

"The back row thinks you're evil."

"Perhaps you could gather in groups of five to
discuss the direct correlation between an increasing
load of electrodynamics homework..."

..."And what?...And what?!"

Holding up a small note, "To answer your request, you have ten minutes for 20% of your grade to broadcast our favorite oscillating electric dipole, and if for some unfortunate reason you could not identify yourself by this most obvious reference you have five minutes. Don't forget to attend your choice of the many inspiring and intriguing seminars on one of which you will base your class presentation, early, not to wait until the last one on the final day lest you become stuck and unbeknownst to your weary and fledgling undergraduate brain cells wind up in Super String Theory. Translation, highly curved double-digit dimensions. Secondary translation, your chances of comprehension relate to the Heavyside $(-x)$ function..."

"Oh," hopeful.

"...for $x > 0$."

"Mmh," lower in pitch, in despair.

"What did static say to the nicely enveloped sinusoidal wavelength?"

"You've been seeing Michelson again, haven't you?"

Maliya clicked at them with an invisible channel changer before sitting down.

Rehearsal was called so the kids could do some

housekeeping and cast their four-inch compressed foam mattresses out to the sun for microbe purging. When the wind kicked up from the burning air even men boasted on themes of laundry loads and just finishing hanging the line only to return to the start without deviation to begin clothes removal. "All we have to do is blockade the neighboring town from terrorists while they're sleeping and an officer is going to periodically take us on jeep tours to replenish our artistic spirit," eating squares of Italian chocolate.

An active soldier from outside the troupe sidled over to Maliya.

"I find you as do my electrons yours," she squashed him into the ground.

"Ooh, repulsive. Nice," the dessert eaters called the play-by-play as Maliya focused on his badge and read off the numbers. It took a bit, but he clued in and vanished before she reached the end.

"That reminds me, do we check our guns by firing downward on the diagonal or into the air?"

"Good point. Descending velocity when the bullet raining from the sky hits people equals its ascending velocity upon leaving the gun shaft, so wouldn't the lobbed bullet stand to injure anyone?"

"At the time it reaches maximum height of its parabolic trajectory it has zero propulsion energy, "zero velocity, so it may descend merely toppling end over end rendering it as dangerous as a rock of similar mass."

"May?"

"Isn't this just a theoretical discussion?"

"We're in the army!"

Chapter Three

Manipulation. Fae was in an army of a different sort. All live in worlds of their own perception, in reflections of the real essence. Images seen are wavelengths not absorbed, but what is an object in the absence of light? Some dodged notice with religious pretense, had their associates questioned about their habits, and were intercepted on that Friday night jaunt to the entertainment district pious no more. Some were channelled through intake by military police and positioned to remote locations, then bolted. Some, after bearing a near suicidal seasoning in the brig, were remanded to special operations. Some.

Relative to that ordeal her commander was disarmingly charming, though is it not the supreme lie to don a desirable character and hide the actual one? Fae was beholden to him...as intended. She was also completely isolated having disengaged through minor rifts and purposeful misunderstandings from those she had met along the way, not discerning that there had always been in the episodes another party involved. And where the puppeteer lacks power to break a bond he'll simply avoid it, perhaps by creating an uncontroversial diversion. So when she was due for spiritual retrieval out popped the amateur psychologist lending diagnosis by his slant, ephemeral foundations of confusion tactics and falsehood relinquishing support of her every step. Suggestions from an underlying motive of control were just blame and belittling disguised. They shrunk Fae to not much of a contender in the next round of unpredictable swings of angry violent outbursts or conversely pathetic appeals for sympathy of perpetrator acting as victim. It was strategic to keep her on edge. Threats, coercion, intimidation, all to exploit weakness. These made light of the emotional abuse inherent in simply picking fights and making accusations. Perhaps her very will and fearlessness blinded her from the hazards of this grooming process of desensitization, as if growing accustomed to a bad neighborhood which would menace any semi-observant outsider, herself included had she been fresh.

However, soon behaviour seemed transparent. Although new facts were not forthcoming Fae's impressions became illuminated with analytic proficiency based on experience, limited cubbyholed options of conduct, and their repetition. She could spot stages by name as he posed there essaying deception: Servility for later gain like pack dogs toward the dominant. Astonishment at the accusation made by the mark in attempt to rid herself of this pest. A fancy-talking transformation to righteous indignation, then fearsome belligerence without flinching. But as she faced him with callous laughter, on to confessions of the obvious regarding transgressions already somewhat public knowledge. Finally, evasion, since the series of ploys failed to yield her compliance yet revealed his weakness extensively. Soldier as an occupation is much more workable nearer the top of the ladder than the bottom, doling misery upon underlings rather than being the recipient. Thus as military culture would have it, the relief of promotion struck Fae no differently. Wielding power versus right, she had the tools. Ally of convenience with the enemy upon a third. Master of the invisible witness to events which didn't exist. G-d of the shadows. Solids touched are not solids at all, merely opposing electrons. And what are these if not energy and space? Everything. Nothing.

"Chk-chk." Fae's head whipped around with bug-eyed inquisitiveness at the close range metal sounds of weapons preparation as a guest accessed their police station under the park.

"It seems there was a break-in at the kibbutz ulpan office," he reported to the moles, duly

concerned, while producing a stack of foreign
passports off his person. He swivelled to view the
suspended monitors which proved to be a contortion
too much as his bunker counterpart with him collided,
spilling forth a separate collection of deceased
Canadians' identities meant for swap. Now the host
klutz was on his knees vaguely dividing both groups
of documents presently strewn on the floor, hastening
to hand up to the unimpressed messenger his intended
pile. "Another one," tersely ordered downward-
reaching palm so it could clasp one more operative
recruit. "Okay, what've you got for me?" shuffling
through the indigo bullion with a rush of nirvana.
"Wait." He consciously respired. "Blessed be their
memories. Sweetest nation over the borders," he
appended glibly. Evidently, the Mossad's proclivity
for maple leaf carrying is inversely proportional to
Canadian olympic athletes', whose refusals meant to
prevent fatigue from marring their upcoming events.
"We need someone to pass for," studying picture and
name, "Anglo-Saxon." Scanning, "You. You can do it
...just stay out of the sun."

And with that the official new persona pat
her, in disbelief contemplating firstly the
discrepancies in accent. Next, assuming a personality.
"What...?"

"...did she do? A regular girl. She ate pizza...in Aza. She strolled in the evening...under Gilo snipers. She drove by bus...along with terrorists...to the bombed disco."

Then lucidity widened her focus to consider what chanced over the time span of the entire visit. "...are the odds that if I toss this into the air the real thing won't catch it?" sarcastically completing her thought.

Penance or just more of the same? Fae was made to analyse tapes sent courtesy of northern enemies featuring Israeli troops disintegrating on booby-trapped roads. "We'll all be in Lebanon soon," Tsomet Patt used to say, who would lie quiet in the fields, gun set to shoot anything that moves as he stared down the shaft for hours until being relieved by his replacement. But films of captives were the worst, the living doomed cheated into tremps off Jerusalem streets by killers dressed as mock orthodox Jews with their shielding facial hair. It was clear he had been beaten, for his lifeless recitation of impossible terms was read by more a poster than a human, a poster owning eyes which twitched upward to their corners for hostile prompts. Hitchhiking entails rules which, the trick notwithstanding, this portrait on her screen had fatefully broken, oral laws pertaining to car type, plates, visibility, driver appearance, speech and demeanor, number of occupants, seating arrangement, and liberty to take action in a spontaneous exit scheme. It was the seventh. He had entered a full vehicle alone. The error could not be undone despite intelligence of his location, even with a raid dynamiting its way into the house, battering through concrete, smothered in cross fire. Both he and a rescuer were shot dead and an entire country went to bed despondent, but not before Fae cleaned up the reporters' version.

From video to trolling live crime scenes. She was to examine, raw, two attack sites. Although one was army, the other a civilian target, the Jordan Valley post and settlement construction booth offensives shared a common element of being manned by unaccustomed Russians, all of whom were murdered by terrorists. And this fact is significant because while their situations appeared innocuous, therein were definite hidden dangers. Remote, resort-like, but one was guarding a porous border. The other sat right beside a city, only, near isn't close enough. A court ruling on the civilian application declared that from then on there must be a minimum of two guards in the Territories at night. Fae reasoned they didn't know where they were.

Loud "kaboom"s rattling windows and activating all car alarms in the city from the air force breezing over low, breaking the sound barrier, ushered in fresh security detail. In a democracy where citizens roam somewhat freely the airport was the place to regain a measure of control. Deciding not to travel they could choose to opt out and leave the building. If, however, the world beckoned, passengers would fall under Fae's scrutiny. "How well do you speak Hebrew?" Her silent pause would indicate whether the wrong response was given. Then the questioning might turn extensive. Cues trained cameras and extra eyes on subjects of interest, and should vacationers not yet be dismayed by the overly sensitive metal detectors they surely did not want to be aware of the complimentary searches and scans of their luggage behind the scenes. Crazed bomb-sniffing mutts in a frenzy were set on the pieces. Ornery tag-flashing hierarchy and protocol. All the suffering war a mad fight against personal demons, pretending they're each other.

Chapter Four

"Aaahhh!" Katamonim walked in the door to find soapy clothes bubbling vicariously in her oversized coffee-maker from a recent bout with lice in which the nation's smallest pet were winning. Not the fact that Ayrden's head was subletting to an exponentially increasing tenant and that the laundry operation was out of control nor that the Kurdish widow herself might be dragged into the circus by one of the better little vaulters was uppermost in her mind, but that her neighbours in the illustrious Sephardic - which just means Spanish, as in the exiles of the Inquisition - ghetto would find out about the unkosher use of a food receptacle to kill vermin, despite that a boiler is self-disinfecting, and wouldn't want to eat at her condo ever again. It wasn't as odd as one might think rooming with a lady that looked like she belonged in one of those old black and white Egyptian movies featured on sixth day afternoons, especially when haggling with the local Arab vendor who was in the habit of setting up her vegetation mini market right on the doorstep. In like havoc, it wasn't long before Ayrden realized that when Katamonim took her ear out she couldn't hear a dashed thing and the stereo could be cranked up as loud as necessary.

Unable to have children, although the jury was out on her late husband, Katamonim would recount the days when chickens ran free range in the house and she perpetually served the spouse and his buddies as they played cards, eating and smoking and drinking beer. "It was a lot of happiness." And she had those quirky superstitions such as hanging to dry wet shoes on cupboard knobs with the soles facing outward was like giving yourself the evil eye...because you're treading on your own face.

    "Do a rotation and look for me there." Jerusalem really was a karma haven. And it's not enough that cretins get theirs, the wronged party inevitably must also gain the satisfaction of finding out that spiritual justice prevailed. Thus, religious girls who turn on each other viciously tend to fling themselves down flights of stairs by chance and gawky display outside the spilling of a toted buffet itself, then return precisely at their friends' departure ...in cast and crutches. Ex-husbands cashing extorted divorce cheques wind up sending forth paperwork relaying tales of injury and unemployment after totalling borrowed cars, those very ones who yanked out television plugs jealous of the cute talk show host Yair Lepid. Is it a wonder that North Americans swapped stories pertaining to which kitchen implements and canned foodstuffs had been damaged in the throes of acting as projectiles targeting their tsabar boyfriends? And don't suppose that when she finally gets rid of him, past quick on his tracks, the fille will have qualms about assisting investigators and the like to his new domicile on the parents' couch.

Ayrden believed in curses. Then again she also impersonated roosters at four in the morning, barked back at the guard dogs of the air base next door before the patrol came - kibbutz living can become monotonous until you find a hobby such as jogging, cookies, walking aimlessly, discussions of cow tipping, and the Israeli boy dormitories - and attempted to teach her Siamese feline that his nips caused actual physical pain via biting him back only to recoil frozen in her fanged expression armed with the newfound knowledge that cats taste terrible. Sort of the flavour you'd expect if you licked a barnyard goat. She fell for it every time the fur ball tormented her new man and then executed a smooth coverup upon her return. He could crawl so slowly his movement was hardly discernible, save progression from one side of the room to the other. He whacked CO detectors and awaited their counterattack. He confiscated microwave ovens in a hissing Karate Kid pose and replaced Ayrden's hello "meow" to greet others with a mere "eh". But be warned: shall no one else take the liberty of touching Sweetie. You just can't buy loyalty like that.

A woman with many bags of produce from the market and even more children conveniently arranged in order of height like steps hands her baby, then stroller, then each successive child and bundles of groceries to the receiving strangers already on the bus. Police and soldiers guard the driver to thwart terrorists grabbing the wheel. Another passenger who could only enter from the middle doors finding himself unable to progress toward the operator past the standing crowds hands a 50 New Shekel bill down the line with the appropriate instructions. Five minutes and ten palms later one adult ticket makes its way back to him along with the correct amount of change. The Egged bus rages down the hill exiting Jerusalem past a semitrailer laden with tanks crawling up so slowly that the soldier accompanying the load is able to walk in front of it miming the pulling of an imaginary rope between himself and the massive vehicle, and past the stone and sand emergency escape ramp engineered on the sinking principle...and the stranded car of the bright-idead Israelis who made the unfortunate mistake of trying it out.

"Come over here. I'd like to speak with you,"

beckoned the thirtyish man behind finger gently
reeling Ayrden to the patio table where he lunched
with another man of similar disposition. "We had
noticed you all the way along this cobblestone road.
You walk like a soldier. Where are you from?" She had
thought nothing of it, although the same had been said
of Eichmann. All the country does service and she
would likely be observed in this manner and receive
like comment again. Or so she thought.

Unlikely was also a word which described a
vast number of purposes for which the army was in
fact useful. During the big Jerusalem snowfall, lacking
salt, snowplows, and electricity, the subsequent state
of emergency called tanks into town to clear the
streets so at least ambulances could reach the
hospitals, never mind employees reaching their jobs or
consumers the stores because work was off and
groceries were not being restocked. In the hot summer
evenings search helicopter gun ships firing around
tank ground support rolling up and down the sandy
flaked-stone hills - built kind of like mille-feuille but in
rock and beach - with the odd whistling flare
descending from the heavens in any one of a multitude
of colours provided an ad hoc sound and light show
for the late night walkers of Maaleh Adomim. Of
course, Tzahal also performed required tasks such as

allowing tourist girls to tour the old city with them during their patrols and teaching them how to use their guns. By the way, if you're offered playtime with a shmuli (meaning "that is opposite me") gun from a horny eighteen-year-old Druze border patrol, decline, if you wish. Israel does know how to exploit its mosaic of talents, though. Under the draft athletes become commandos, intellectuals are educated for specified positions, survivalist manipulators turn into undercover operatives, and rejects on all of the above counts get to run the base concession stand.

Russian immigrants were quiet unobtrusive neighbours that you'd carry on heartened conversations with outside the building not realizing that they lived in the apartment right beside you. It was the same with the Chinese in Toronto, or anyone from a regime where people disappeared in the middle of the night. They had the fear. Mind you, the General Security Service of the Hebraic variety had also been known to detain in secret its own citizens for such outspoken remarks as "...and it was snatched up faster than a ship full of uranium off the coast of Israel" because officially the country was not the fourth largest superpower in nuclear weaponry. Upon primary absorption to the kibbutzim the Eastern Blockers would be observed stuffing themselves with the entire selection of foods from both the hot and cold cafeteria trolleys. In time this habit died down, when came the realization that large quantities of any given meal did not necessarily imply that there would not be food at the next scheduled mealtime, as perhaps was the case in their country of origin. But, surprisingly, they excelled at the art of standing in line. They would legitimately hold places in multiple queues simultaneously by requesting that others around them maintain their spots, only to reappear abruptly and slightly infuriatingly in each line as their turns came up. Now this did not sit well with the natives who were insistent that everyone suffer equally. Theoretically, if the doctor was an hour behind schedule it was not advisable to call ahead for this information and arrive accordingly late, estimating when your appointment would truly take place since you'd inevitably wind up exchanging words with someone who in her own brand of perverted logic would rather you'd sweat it out in the seat next to her. Theoretically.

The Ethiopian immigration in the form of covert naval operation Shlomo was much more dramatic. Having travelled on foot and by truck from designated checkpoint to checkpoint for weeks on pure faith that they were to be brought to Jerusalem they finally made it to a mock seaside resort owned by A in the name of B in the name of C, etc., until at the end of the long pseudo list was the state of Israel, standing behind a tree. During the demanding journey where babies died of dehydration they were under constant threat of discovery and capture by mercenaries and at the shore the Israelis faced heated gunfire while awaiting their passengers' arrival to the boat. The second operation was by plane. Lod's tarmac erupted with cheers as black Jews draped in white flowing sheets looking like they had just walked off the pages of the Torah descended from the jumbo. But rising up to the land of goats' milk and dates from any foreign culture only to immediately be drafted into a game of war with yet unfamiliar rules is also a quick way to wind up deceased.

"I'm ready to tour Israel," stated Ayrden's dad. He had his shirt untucked and a scowl on his face. She reminded him to drive speedily in the Territories at night, not to allow an unknown car to come alongside, but to definitely stop for the army barricade because if he ran it they would fire. "Trespassers will be shot!" he emphasized recalling the English translation of the sign at the central Tel Aviv military base. They didn't much appreciate the concept of u-turn on their driveway by a bunch of tourists.

Israelis' preoccupation with security does have advantages over the open western society in some respects. The fact that terrorists find children an irresistible target results in guarded gated schools inaccessible to drug pushers and social predators as an added bonus although the parents pay for this service themselves, meaning, the guarding. The others come free. All garbage is stowed away in large removable containers or in locked common rooms, never left smelling curbside for individual pickup as this is an excellent hiding place for explosives. Failure to adhere to this policy and, say, forget at the bus stop your bag of junk snacks for the class party will be cause for street closure and the deployment of the bomb squad, complete with detonating robot, a loud "BOOM!"... and chips everywhere. Mandatory army service is also good for shaking the natural rhythm out of crazy teens and forming clean-cut fortyish twenty-year-olds with just the degree of uniformity comfortable to a socialist society, that is, when they don't kill themselves or refuse and spend their conscription years in jail.

Chapter Five

"And we're brainstorming...skits, concepts, inspiration. Bring it forth, company."

"Excuse me," a female voice ventured.

"No, you're not fat," assured Maliya.

"How did you...? Thank-you."

"Improv, what post are you manning these days?" exploring avenues of interest.

He scrapped with empty chairs in a mad dash out.

"Jingle for animal control:

So come take 'em home if they've run away,
before we kill them. We are your pound.
All the cute little animals...
lethal injection. Doo doo doo.

A wee squad signalled themselves to action. Incandescent lamps strobed. Rock music pulsed. A girl in fatigues removed her hair band and shook her locks, prancing as a runway model. She then spoofed a catalogue photo, posing and pointing off to the corner. Two males sauntering over in like fashion witnessed her, glanced at each other, and spontaneously joined the pose to stare where she goggled. Lighting guy stopped flickering the switch for a blackout. The music faded.

"Tss," Comedian ambushed from behind, pretending to depress a foam canister's nozzle, the real object of fear.

His target leapt from the sound, in a frenzy checking herself for residue.

"I know! Let's play Solid Gold dancers," flagging attention from further over by waving maniacally.

"Let's not," rejected the opposite corner of the room aping the fanning limb motion.

"We could invent a three-dimensional jigsaw puzzle of planet Earth. Continents, oceans, atmospheres, landmarks, flora and fauna as singular pieces. No. The universe."

"Fear Factor paraplegic style!"

"Oh! The disabled piano duo 'Three arms and four hands'."

Illustrator murmured a joint venture pitch to Morose Writer, "...and the baby animals travel around the world having crazy adventures."

"It could work, if they were really big scary babies with fangs that look at you and freeze your brain so you never wake up," clawing a Godzilla impression.

"That's not what I was going for in a preschooler nappy time picture book."

Overhearing, "Writer's block? Use a definition. The eyes did not melt but changed state from a solid to a liquid."

"You're just jealous of my fictional characters," Morose backlashed.

"There's no secret to creating art if you're egotistical," pausing to realize she had in fact insulted herself.

"What about you?" prodding a spectacled studious one with nose in a manual.

He closed and set it down, responding blankly, "I only talk about what I know," before resuming with the volume as earlier, save one glimpse across his glasses' brim. Then back to the page.

"Get this," Morose marketed. "Never screw over the Terror Tools," he warned creepily, "'cause they'll come a charge to unhinge you!"

"It's still a children's novel."

"So you've got nothing. Bring on the periodic table superheroes."

Maliya scurried up:

Once there is a thought as to what
reality is, it is so...

The gallery was disquieted. "Deep."
Slapping his head, "What does that even mean?"

In a parallel existence occupying the same time-space as our own lives Speedfree the spinning master of the universe and his Defense Army of Valence.

"Like it. Don't know why."

The configuration of his world is not one that we know but a block of 109 planets and their orbiting 1-109 moons, respectively, all hovering stationary in an unnoticeable square of darkness. It is thus known to the inhabitants as The Dark System, for its central point and for its character. Life here is volatile. The members are bombarded daily. And aside from the unified steadfast and loyal Defense Army of Valence operating on each planet's outermost moon shell it is very much everyone for himself.

"Sounds familiar."

On a regular basis weak All Killed,
Aye's metal is tested as it is left
thieved of a defender by positively
righteous Hall of Guns conquerors, as
evident in the salt wars when powerful
chlorine annexed sodium into its empire.

"Warning. Warning. Rust attack. Oxygen
pillages iron."

And there is something that no one
wants you to discover, a region beyond
the Hall of Guns stronghold, isolated
planets of peace settled by the closed
gaseous aristocracy. While The Dark
System battles and loots, these Nobles
remain inert floating their own interests
such as conductorless streetcars and
nondegrading infrastructure while
having lawyers impose a news blackout
on their status.

"It's nice to at least hear the topic before
we're told the crazy story."
"What was this supposed to be about, again?"
"Does it matter?"
"So elementary."

In the beginning the block was created
in seven periods with Speedfree its
essence.

"I knew it!" praised Religious.
"Shielded moons were in line buying a ticket
for coach when the price suddenly plummeted for
first class," a student proudly continued.
"Not you, too."

And thus the prophecy was fulfilled
that when planets are listed in rows
ordered by the number of their moons,
similar chemical and physical properties
recur at regular intervals.

"I always marvel how she gets that from that."
"The professor only has two speeds: fast
forward and reverse, but no play."

But moons aren't particles...

"No!"

...rather pure streams of energy clouds
filling entire orbital volumes, being
everywhere at once.

"Don't superheroes require an archrival, you
know, to mix it up a little?"
"I thought this was almost over."
"Evil Auntie Speedfree..."
"...and her two limping stepsisters."
"Relatives can be so repellent."
"Yet they manage to suck you in."
"Well stated."
"It's my natural magnetism."
"I don't get it."

Spinning Speedfree in his perfection
would keep the system aligned and
neutralized. But incomplete, he is
subject to various degrees of crooked
influence from the family and planet-
moon placement is destabilized and
distanced, accounting for the open

vulnerability of the left vis-à-vis the
right. All Killed, Aye suffers most from
the witches' spell 'I'll tilt ya, the Hun'.

"Does that have anything to do with science, I
askew?"

"No. I'm subbing social studies next. And so
are noticeable the effects of continuums, dimensional
or information, causing one reality to collide with
another.

Such is the sisters' legacy. None shall
ever forget.

"While on topic I would convey Pauli's principle had
I not already done so with the class ahead of yours,"
gathering her notes and evacuating the stage.

"What's a six-letter excellent killing machine?"
an inattentive one puzzled.

"German."

"Come on."

"Does French cheese smell?"

"That's my answer and I'm sticking to it."

"I liked the Dutch. They were nice, sweet."

"Before handing over all the Jews to the
Gestapo."

"They probably told their kids that their little friends of the Book were off to a better life on a farm."

"Ah, my juvenile delinquent neighbour was shipped to kibbutz...She came back, eventually."

"Did she? Do they ever, really?"

"Why are you doing the crossword when there are usable articles here?" rifling through the paper for material. "'With the police at the door a suspect decided to take refuge in his fridge in the hope of eluding them. Seeing food and shelves strewn on the kitchen floor, however, alerted the cops to the man's hiding place which they promptly checked out. Upon opening the door they caught him with the light bulb in his hand which he claimed to be changing and such was the reason for his presence there.'"

"Yeah, I always replace the bulb that way."

"He might have been removing it so they wouldn't see him in the dark."

"You think? The remedial army is down the hall."

"You could've fooled me."

"There is no hall."

Chapter Six

"Allaaah..." Arabic prayers broadcast over the land by loudspeaker to Fae resounded of a war cry. Don't interact. Observe. Assess. Be a disinterested third party, not the object of focus. Only without interference can a proper opinion be formulated on the situation, and it is then when the matter is settled that others should be informed, not before. Both Fae and Maliya had joined the forces, but just one was presently being snuck out the back door into Jordan. Senses wired keen, a product of her training. Fae's mind raced back and forth between then and now.

"Once a unit traversed the country on foot..." the legend began, so from then on everyone combat-ready would be required to duplicate the feat, a prime example of the exception becoming the general rule. Haven't they heard hard cases make bad laws? Stride. Stride. It follows that a sandal-clad population exercising in flat boots should be without arches. The gruelling schedule was not as some testify the manifestation of beating down individuals so as to rebuild them into a military team, rather slogging the body until extraneous thoughts cease for they have a knack of pestering one to the point of inaction. Strive to react in spontaneity. Push your perceived limits.

Create the realm of the possible. It's all very Zen. Stride. Stride. Awaken an instinctive surviving animal. For what you yet are not certain, keep a belly of faith. Faith? That's it? An associate on this mission indeed cut open his parachute when it failed to deploy, with a knife, mid free fall. Another was a specialist in passing in and out of Aza like a sand-saturated desert wind. His bravado raved that when insurgents visualize the Israelis descending upon them they're struck with fear. Conditioning. Relinquish that frontal lobe to the telltale stare of indoctrination. Canada takes the opposite tack by crouching below the radar.

A shot was fired. The group took heed. A Jordanian soldier had spontaneously misfired. Too much Zen. Fae beamed at him with relief, stealing attention from her agitated male compatriots. Last week in the Jerusalem dorms a stray bullet from a student engaged in gun-cleaning had flown through his door and across the hallway, penetrating a second door and sadly the university student occupying that other room. All the cold field showers and boot camp in tents because new immigrants flooding the country were in need of the base's regular living quarters, all the toughening didn't save him. Staggered access might have. Conditioning, not so much.

More a surgical strike than an invasion, akin to

a guided rocket weaving about city structures in downtown Beirut until the final corner is turned, ascension to the next floor, now into the bomb-maker's apartment straight through his window. Though, Fae's trio aimed to substitute explosion with poisoning and they had prepared for such by sprinting through the streets of Tel Aviv and pitching glasses of water on people. "You're carrying that blade? It extends past four finger widths. Not legal," contended Aza.

And assassination is, pondered Fae.

"My lucky cutter." Red Boots was offended. Remeasuring, "I guess that depends on how puny your tiny hands are. Looks lawful from up here." Speaking to Fae, "Stand by, second date."

"Third time, ice cream."

She breezed past the recurring Jordanian soldier with physical neglect and spiritual focus. Snared him.

Sweeping the crush of Amman's bustling market and café district, "Bull's-eye kept his appointment."

"Intelligence wasn't able to gather more witnesses?"

"Horde of cover, chaos, diversion." They made after their terrorist through the maze and impasse of stalls and people until the interception, casual to the point of uneventful. Then to pursue the decoy, in need of some reeling in. Seeming a lone female tourist Fae had captivated a bothersome huddle of renegade patrol, so invoking the art of improvisation her two counterparts boldly as locals approached the suitors for a face to face to apprise them in Arabic of the hubbub in the city centre. The dilemma was that for the short term gain of releasing Fae the authorities had been informed of an attack on an unidentified man in a known location, but the target himself was still unaware he'd been hit. In having attention drawn to the crime the wanted man would pay heed to his deteriorating health, find the piercing, and realize it came from one miniscule lethal dart soon enough to seek treatment. Furthermore, the textbook pretty girl and two men with prior knowledge had all laid themselves bare before foreign security with propitious timing, placement, and purpose. They were caught at the border within the hour reentering Israel.

And there was a twist. While Jordanian officials soberly outlined the nature of the restraint being suspicion of attempted murder, each of the three isolated in custody and currently responding to interrogators in off-toned English stubbornly refused assistance from the embassy of Canada. Diplomats made efforts to visit their citizens held abroad all the same, so the Canucks did become involved. As such their disclosure that the bearers of these Canadian passports were in fact not entitled to do so came bittersweet. On one hand the actors were agents of the Mossad disregarding foreign law and jurisdiction in an antiterrorist elimination plot. On the other hand the actors were agents of the Mossad disregarding foreign law and jurisdiction in an antiterrorist elimination plot. Subsequently, Canadian ambassadors in Tel Aviv holidayed from their post for a whole week in protest of the wrongful use of their flag, not believing their fortune that the scandalous characters were not nationals after all.

The Israelis ultimately were traded back over the river in a squeeze for the antidote. "How did she perform?"

Fae's commander offered report to his own superior, "The girl was on track, disciplined to protect her identity. Had she been left alone, maybe stayed on to tour Petra, she'd have remained clear of the mess."

"It was the others?"

"They were being protective."

"By implicating her and wasting a slew of resources?"

The commander fathomed the unholy bond between higher-ups and his underling, more so since he and Fae shared a similar odd devoted-oppressive acquaintance. He would have broke cover to save her too. He could never have just let her go. Commitment. Alas the commander had overlooked that it also flows the other way and that offenders have fear, meaning an assertive resistance will thwart crime so long as the transgressor hovers in the gray testing area and has not yet committed. Doubt cannot champion, and that is why in contact fighting his students could never win. They feared injury. The opposition reads how far a person has himself resolved to go. A foe will believe solely to the extent that you do.

Fae was dissecting traces of a longtime prisoner fighter pilot in Iran. Summoned from a sweaty tall-shadow basketball scramble to the air base cuddling his home and on to Lebanon, he had often proceeded thus, in fact usually returning to the kibbutz court within the hour. Howbeit, the duration flipped to biblical scale when his craft was shot down. He ejected but that's where fortune ended. Cage sized for a coffin in eternal night. Sentenced to a pit of filth crawling and slithering. Starvation. Dehydration. Torture. Lebanon. Syria. Iran.

"We got The Engineer!"

Elation burst from the crevices of electronic gadgets where the operators hid. Finally, success. The Engineer, as he was designated, was not a bona fide engineer, merely a principal explosive device manufacturer in Aza. Dozens of killings lay on his head. He was much sought. So stingers punctured his circle to switch his cellular phone with their upgraded model, elevated to the highest degree. Everything set in place, what was left to do but call him, gun ships hovering above the site? A blast. No more Engineer. That was all the public was told, leaving them wondering whether the phone had been configured to a frequency to detonate his own homestead chemical stockpile, whether it was the transmitter itself which was stuffed with sufficient explosive material to take off his head, or if the telephone's function was just voice recognition and relaying the destination coordinates for a missile. Small victory. Another would take his place. Death cycles on.

Chapter Seven

Speaking of ex-in-laws who cite not winding up in the clink among their family's great accomplishments although some did become policemen, Ayrden could recall one particular Shabbat meal with those squabbling siblings when a macaroni tray stopped short of her husband, dumping an extra large load on the plate of his mother who upon realizing the oversight promptly sans utensils grabbed a handful of her pasta and plonked it on the table in front of him. She was readying her tomatoey fingers for a second go but was vehemently encouraged not to by the rest of the diners in one spontaneous gesture of excitedly outstretched hands and voices in unison imploring, "No!" And the thing about a cross-cultural relationship with a psychologist's dream family is that after you stop laughing they start to get really irritating. Sure, while name-calling tirades, endless criticism, and furniture punching can be entertaining coming from another language, century, and species, when you run out of putty you realize that one just shouldn't spit in the well that one drinks from.

And that was the night of the watcher. They dispersed to their respective apartments but a particular group stumbled upon the presence of an

intruder, the trespasser on the roof of the level
beneath which doubled function as an enormous
balcony since it stood right off a window and flimsy
screen door. It was the roommate who discovered
him. Unknowingly, she nonchalantly conversed with
the man in the shadows under the mistaken
assumption he was Ayrden's mate just stepped out
for a smoke. However, this fantasy of denial fearfully
shattered when replies resounded not from the object
in her vision but the adjacent room, where Ayrden and
the real partner were carrying on and had been so
doing well before she returned home. So he was
spying them. And nothing had been stolen. Even with
three occupants interrupting his intrigue he coolly
stayed, leaning into the wall, smoking. Only the
roommate's alerting screams finally drove him up a
ladder to the next roof and away. Ayrden made a
mental note to toss said ladder the following day.

Rapidly developing a distaste for people.
Spontaneous encounters popping up. The mystics are
back, searching their messiah, denouncing the country
that provides their shelter. What now? Carrying a
symbolic rose? Messages written on her forehead?
Looking like David? Wow, they must be some kind of
geniuses with their psychic impressions...since we're
all really one. Trying to leave. Try harder. In an

unearthly gesture the beautiful guy accompanying on foot a long red Mercedes with its usual fifty passengers as it turned past the old city abruptly twisted his gaze into its tinted window at the girl concealed on the inside whose eyes had been treading the pavement with his mysterious figure. He sensed it. He was also a monk. Down the road in the centre of town a handsome Yemenite decided his shirt needed a second tuck into his jeans. Not lacking in self-confidence, suddenly pants dropped below Hawaiian boxers effecting smiles and much tooting from all who drove by his bus stop. Meanwhile at the clinic a dentist revelling in the cocoa break he was receiving thanks to a no-show was pretending to shoot up with a previous patient's needle. As he changed his shirt the female office manager opened and hurriedly shut the door in embarrassment for having entered not realizing that his dental assistant, resident voyeur, was also in the room providing background striptease humming. "Ayrden! You have five hundred messages," her boss shrieked at her upon returning from a month long vacation during which guess who was in charge of that section of the five star hotel?

Not too sure of its fate in the west, Red's fairground video was certainly a big hit in Jordan on

par with Ricky Martin's Maria and Khaled's Didi.
Israel enjoys Argentinean soap operas, Spanish with
Hebrew subtitles. In fact, subtitles become so
addictive that one tends to read television even when
the program is in one's native tongue, exposing
translation errors on the side. But saving money
spurred the creative solution of homegrown political
talk shows on such typical topics as "Are we in for
war on any of our fronts?", "Did the public official
err, lie, commit a criminal act, or send a hit squad on
an ally and bungle it causing an international
spectacle?", and "Are we in an economic depression?"
to which one may respond that if it's preferable to fill
airtime this way than to buy a hit American comedy
the answer is yes.

Don't expect the local news to inform you of
extra high ambient radiation levels because of an
undisclosed event at the desert nuclear power station,
though. You'll have to tune in over the border for that
tidbit. In Israel censorship is its own industry, but
there are some common threads to it. Forego
uprooting outright lies per se, save the odd
surreptitious moving of a ceasefire fence in the dead of
night, unlike the baseless to reckless inflammations of
the surrounds spewing "We will wipe you off the
planet!" Well, that one might be true. If veritably

caught, matters merely claim status of being "still under investigation". Middle Easterners of the area tend to try one on over a perceived weak group, but when backed into a corner they also may quickly back down since a power play isn't a winning one when the other side knows what you're up to and is game. Why can't the western politician just admit his guilt and stoically face impending legal remedies when the jig is up? There's something to be said for the chap that "did it" in this era when prisons purport to all be packed with the criminally innocent. Television is used as an effective propaganda tool promoting nationalism where even entertainment films contain the popular "everyone in the entire world hates us" motif, but media must strike a delicate balance between communicating the dire predicament of the country's citizens and actually frightening them into exile. When the Jewish race isn't a part of the program, often it refreshingly is chosen to be the resilience of the human spirit, pioneering, or reaffirming priorities. There is always contained in it a message. Nevertheless, one does relish not wasting time viewing TV fast food...as he pays the hefty broadcast tax...and a fee for radio too. Religious sensitivities can be depended upon by all to monitor content and preserve a modicum of conservatism, when the ultra-orthodox aren't too busy setting the advertisements inside bus stops on fire. Getting used to the aforementioned and relatives across the Atlantic informing you by phone where the bombs fell in your own neighborhood, the only remaining misuse of the airwaves is the state-designated mourning day which seems to be enacted much too frequently. No matter which station is selected everything on radio will be folk tunes or appropriately depressing slow popular songs. That is how it is. Resistance just increases the discomfort.

"Moshe! Throw the keys," bellows a man in the parking lot to the fourth storey of a white marble building.

"I can't find them," returns a voice from above.

"In the pants. And there's a twenty in the pocket. Bring me."

"I found, but how do you want me to throw a bill?"

"Throw."

"Like that?"

"Throw!"

Meanwhile back at the Faculty of Law where professors hand back papers complete with spelling corrections for the foreign students, where writing in multiple languages is tolerated in keeping with judicial tradition and often resulting in changing directions mid-sentence, you must jump into the air and wave your arms every few minutes if studying alone in a lecture hall in order to reactivate the conservational motion sensing lights. And in the open market the bra salesman looks at your chest matter-of-factly and declares that you are size number five which he then extricates from the pile along with the bikini underwear you requested as he demonstrates the quality of its elastic and you remind yourself to wash everything thoroughly when you get home. Around the corner a youth without a token dials the rotary phone by hanging up rhythmically to the numbers. "Believe me, doll. Don't believe anyone." On a step in the sun out of the way of the crowds a girl strokes her boyfriend's hair, his head dozing in her lap, when his pal motions he'll take over, the gentle caresses turning haphazard over the face, becoming slaps.

"You 'ave dy-sen-te-ry," diagnosed the Aussie doc at the Red Star of David first aid station in his best Middle Easterner speaking English accent after being told that his patient only understood Hebrew. "Tayke won peel ev'ry too ow-ers," he continued to mime with fingers in the air and pointing to his watch. Another fine example of precise interlingual medical

care. Patient soon made that look - I have to see
Migeo - and was down the hallway again.

Two Arabs enter a t-shirt shop on Son of
Yehuda Street, one handing a photo of what looked
like a live mummy complete with semiautomatic
weapon and matching ammunition necklace accessory
to the store clerk as the other revealed a gun under his
jacket. "I mean, I can see the look you're going for,"
joked the Brazilian dentist turned chef attempting not
to die by way of levity, "but if you were to have your
picture taken couldn't you just put on a nice shirt like
everyone else?...Why not?"

"Why so?" shrugged the voice of the Israeli
tentative in the corner.

Chapter Eight

"You don't have to need a cup of tea," Maliya sassed. "Maximum you get up and go pee pee and the whole process starts again. Where's the disaster? Who died from that? Cake?"

"Mmm, sodium carboxymethylcellulose," Musician complimented. "I'm seeing a model."

"Limping guy has really got muscular degenerative disease in his eyes," examining the room inquisitively.

"Not here, right now," explaining. "Ah, the falling. What's he doing for that?"

"Training a dog. You've got to be careful out there. You don't want the gift that keeps on giving."

"Tall ones stiffen my neck."

"It all evens out horizontally. Hey, a person can claim a disability amount if he is 'certifiably blind all or almost all of the time'," quoting the Tax Is Your Friend docket.

"'Let go of the side,' said my hunky swimming instructor when I was young." Sarcastically, "'You can trust me.'"

"Uh huh."

"And that was the beginning of the end."

"Speaking of which, I don't get the deal with

"that commercial where the brand new car sits motionless, alone, in the middle of the longest bridge in Canada over the ocean. Yeah, I want that car."

"How is that 'speaking of which'?"

"Bygones," brushed off Maliya. "Do my make-up?"

"Before you know it, they're backing up so much you swear you hear beeping."

Improv jarred their girl talk with his presence. "And I would like to thank broccoli," ladle replacing microphone.

"Can you make me beautiful?" Repressing the mocker, "You be quiet."

"I wasn't going to touch that."

"The moment he sees you he's running to purchase a return ticket."

"If you expect an award you'd better get out the papier-mâché. There."

"Go back for another hour."

"Gorgeous. Don't hate me," adoring the mirror.

"Oh, not to worry," he condescended.

"Ingrained in your head, footsteps tearing away." Musician's outbursts crescendoed to a natural peak.

"Relax. There don't exist two words more

"awful than vertical linoleum."

"You know, when a person sends me a chapter it should be chapter one. Some people messenger chapter eight, and I don't have a clue who these characters are or what on earth is happening. And one hundred and twenty pages is not a novel."

"Novella! You said it had potential," Morose whipped, overhearing. "I couldn't very well flower on about that DVD you did. Satirical artists' conversations? Really."

"Ah! It was a hyperbole."

"Watch these old actors shift facial flesh around as they smooch in this movie."

"Ugh. There's a reason for retirement."

"At least they shouldn't press so hard."

"Blur. Blur. Please add blur."

"No good can come from perfect strangers mistaking you for a lesbian."

"Not to fret, I've always revered the study of Shakespeare."

"That's thespian."

"I see, so you limit your focus to the more obscure Elizabethan scribes?"

"Now that you mention it, I had a friend who actually was. Truly, not me. Okay, he was my boyfriend. Well, he was graced with passion and "sensitivity, and yes, the leather pants and cowboy boots should have been a dead giveaway like the air holes in the container of illegal immigrants, but that's not the point here."

"Which is?"

"I have a suspicion that is precisely how he wound up in the myriad of drama courses at college after filling out an extremely personal computerized form to assist in determining a major. We're deferrals. He'd put in gay-slash-lesbian, altogether one option, and they'd give him Othello. Admittedly at the time we didn't quite get the connection although his term papers were very interesting."

Mime ranted into the congregation, "That dirt on the worm in the mess inside Mahmud's donkey's butt."

"Who?"

"Who else? Him, that's who."

"Oh, him. How is he, dear?"

Improv couldn't resist injecting fuel, "You're a sweetheart, no matter what they say about you."

"They say things about me?"

"I just threw that in to make you completely neurotic."

"Interested in the science experiment conducted by a Moroccan family?"

Arousing setup. "Do tell."

"It involved the expenses incurred for constant versus varying use of current based on the direct correlation of cost to efficiency and the premise that the transient surge when flipping the switch might prove more wasteful than leaving the power on."

"In Israel?"

"Operating which appliance?"

"A high-intensity electric water heater..."

"Oh no."

"...located on the roof of the building, in winter."

"The idea is applicable for a light bulb!"

"Minor substitution on the basic physical equation."

"It presupposes a frequency of use equivalent to constant," continuing to obsess.

"The brothers' interpretation was closer to one sixth."

"But the energy output could be measured by simply reading wattage usage over a period as short as a few seconds. Seconds!" wildly wheezing the repeat.

"They thought they'd just wait for the bill."

"How long was that?" inquisitive lucidity danced in between.

"Does the news coverage mean anything?"

"Ah." Turning to the nervous one, "Don't you have guard duty?"

Like an animal he escaped the structure believing himself late for a crucial function.

"He does not..."

"No."

"Did you hear they're making fridges and stoves now with GPS's?"

"For all those weekends off when they enjoy a jaunt to the water?"

"Anything come of participating in regression therapy at the university?"

"Stam hoax. Money for nothing," yet he traversed the chamber curiously sidestepping, back-stepping, twisting with bent knee and rhythmic lilt.

"Nach. You've nev'r bin there," countered a manufactured Gaelic accent to the impromptu Hebraic folk dances.

An announcement was made. "People, I put somebody's wet bra over the radiator so they won't wake up tomorrow and have cold breasts all day."

"Thanks." By the baritone expression of gratitude it appeared there was a slight discrepancy as to the undergarment's rightful owner.

"On the subject, would Dancer care to zip up?" Snapping, "And take it out of third."

"Since that's where the girls' attention is concentrated," lazily reaching to make the adjustment.

Baritone's voice crept in again, "Not a problem," somehow speeding the process.

Morose pinned Musician with claims of defamation, "You know in that girl-talk sketch I was the guy you described as 'icky'. You can't do that."

"Oh yeah. But I wasn't even talking about you. Next time I put a disclaimer."

"The only thing that wasn't true was the disclaimer. And what do you mean by 'oh yeah'?"

"'T' hell with liability. If you recognize yourself being badmouthed, it is you."

"Not politically correct," censors grumbled.

"Come on. I joked about barbaric exes. I didn't do a Mel and recrucify Yeshu."

"I always wondered whether my exes were reluctant to shower with me because I urinated from upstream or if it was due to the searing water and eye-stinging soap steam."

"That could've been it."

"Note to self," marked a bystander.

"My family isn't attending my wedding."

"Or you could have my sister's ceremony where the members line up stalely beside those they find least reprehensible among the bunch, straining "smiles like this." He illustrated with a soulless toothy half-faced example. "Oh, you have a white hair," honing in. "I was going to pluck it, but where would it end?"

"As one ages the rule is to gather the hair around the face to lessen its severity."

"There's also enshrouding."

"Plastic surgery," came a suggestion.

"Line bulimia? If you're going to live your life you'll have a face that shows it. You'd mutilate yourself for fear of time? Look! It's a watch. Boohoohooahh!" Maliya dreadfully thrust her wrist at them.

"Aaah!" they yelped, momentarily caught in the horror of the device.

"I like dodge ball. It was the only sport in gym I could play as a kid."

"Which explains why you're a soldier in the arts company."

"You don't have to hit the ball, or maneuver it with any fancy skill. You just run away."

"I'm throwing my hat into the ring."

"Isn't that gloves?"

"And what sort of a ring is it anyway?"

"Maliya, what do you have to say?"

"Don't accept a gift cellphone if there is an

"Israeli helicopter flying overhead."

"Illuminating."

"Is it video? 'Cause I wouldn't want to pass on picturephone."

"For the purpose of being on the same page let's just say it's plain old audio."

"Cool. A gift cellphone."

Chapter Nine

Fae waded blindly through the ink air of late hours up the base drive, sandals reading brailled concrete to keep from tripping off the edge. It was safer backpacking in darkness than on the partially lit Jordan Valley highway behind her. Arab cars had a tendency of striking Jewish pedestrians. Perhaps she could have encountered snakes or scorpions if her countrymen didn't slather on the poisons. Silent black, like dreaming awake. Conscious experience frail as it be is no more acceptably real than the mind's travels during sleep. Why would the unconscious theatre resign itself to messaging when it could just be? A lone light at the booth. Fae trotted past the guard there posted who was alert for perimeter infiltrators, as if nothing was unusual. The idea is that no one can harm one who creates a world free of danger. Different from ignorance, this is a self-fulfilling state of thought and energy. It also didn't hurt that Fae was on the move, whereas the guard had been stationed like furniture. To spy him is to know him then assail his weakness.

Another death threat on her phone. By the words he had chosen he knew her. Organized mayhem was overtaking the country as its largest union revolted against government policy and shut down business communications, customer service of private monopolies, and the airport. The army machine contributed its fair share, embarking on a confiscation policy of civilian possessions it wanted for itself. At last glance a family's imported all-terrain SUV was ordered to reserve duty.

A prank call aimed to lure Fae from secured grounds. Estimated travel time to the proposed destination would suffice for a raid on her flat. At the very least the tour would run her around needlessly, for the bag she was purported to have lost in town blotted her table even as they conversed. Hours earlier Fae had graced that spot where he claimed she had mislaid her belongings and so requested her return, but the work was sloppy and he gave a numerical address which didn't match the taxi stand but was kitty-corner to it. Neither did the name correspond to that company. Some person had placed her in the vicinity and rattled off objects found there, shop types, visible numbers, none having anything to do with the other. He guessed that taxis in the city centre would be called Central Taxis, which they weren't. What is more, allegations of obtaining her dialing information from a bill contained in the present missing pouch meant she was being surveilled. Fae did pay that bill some blocks away at the sole post office operating over the strike. "Don't go," advised well-meaning strangers. In Israel there are a lot of these. "Anyway, you cannot just perform as a liar craves."

Next, the police held a statement against her and without divulging its content demanded an appearance at the nearby station. Perplexity matured into anxiety. "Have you rowed with anyone lately?" Fae's commander asked rhetorically. "That's who it is, must be."

"So a guy who's mad goes clear across town and falsifies testimony to the authorities because he's got an hour to kill?"

"Guilty people often point fingers. Panic. Thwarting suspicion. Multiple hit rule. You can attend the police session. They've got nothing. Should you be surprised, though, close your mouth. But the telephone meeting, I don't like that at all. What if you show up and someone hands you a sack full of drugs before it sets in that this isn't yours?"

That had not been on her list of possibilities. Fae knew who she had riled, her primary suspect on the bag issue. Two sides of the same coin. When a man seeks to trust another he will describe him as decent, but that same honest man to a con is viewed as gullible. The disparity of approach does not disprove that these are both characteristics of one man. In fact they are complementary. That Fae had been engaged in dialogue with the prankster moments prior to his ruse strengthened this deduction, howbeit counterintuitive. Untruth rang even then between the acquaintances. Perhaps the key was not in words uttered, rather the pauses.

The commander contacted his superior. "Enough. Stop flexing." Practice was one thing. Why torment her mind with dirty tricks so she's brainwashed into striking the world before it hits her? What program was he on? Wait and the girl will be him. She was drilled to protect her identity. He would never let her go.

"That's okay. I don't need to feel my knees," Fae responded to questions regarding her comfort when viced into the rear compartment of their jeep. This evening renounced closure.

Fingers from somewhere pinched skin on the back of her hand momentarily under flashlight. She and the instigator peered at its sluggish retraction. "Dry," he commented. "Drink water," transferring a canteen, "all of it." The vehicle pressed ahead in the oven wind.

Here. Destination hijacking. A bus. Military.
Ambulances. Small town of passengers. The heat of
the conflict had been suppressed and control restored,
so why the garbage crew? One of the gunmen had
been sniped to start the commando race on the scene.
Civilian victims mobbed number two, en masse
delivering fist blows until he expired. Soldiers devoid
of the manpower to arrest them, prosecutors unable
to charge a large traumatized group without criminal
files who committed homicide as a result only of the
combined contributions of each and every component
member. None was singly responsible so it was to
imprison all of them - the parents, youths, old ladies
who tossed a mean rock - all of them or none. Number
three was caught alive. Precisely. Despite the
judiciary constituting a zealous warrior for the rule of
law in utopia where they resided, the midst of battle
had the executive arm brandish implements of survival
with a tad more pragmatism. This conflict meant that
in greater numbers soldiers were held accountable for
unlawful killings, circumstances where the hostile had
been immobilized yet the order was still given.
Successive caution thus wrought the necessity for
cleaners, those who would follow the Prime
Minister's instructions regarding terrorists captured
living. They didn't exist.

The commander made a point of intersecting Fae as she crossed the base sometime after dawn. "Dry," he said while squeezing her skin as she tugged away her hand impatiently. "Drink water."

"What?" stormed Fae, exhausted.

He had been stewing. "I want you to hear me clearly in what I'm about to relate."

"Like the board breaking lessons when you assured it wouldn't sting and my entire body pulsed with that wicked dulled needle sensation?"

"Don't ever allow a circumstance where you cannot protect yourself."

Pivoting away irreverently, "Besides that statement being slightly redundant in our line it is also antithetical to permit chance."

His snatch froze her. "It is possible to be able to decide on a course of action which will render you functionally disabled."

"Ah, you're a short leash advocate," scorching his hand with mere gaze. "If I didn't want someone to bite me I'd opt to keep him on the far end loop of one of those long poles."

He withdrew before she came through on the threat. "You heard me," earnestly demanding attention.

No matter what.

Chapter Ten

Past midnight. She has just cuddled up into bed. The engine of a snow blower blurts its noisy cacophony into sleeping ears of thousands of residents of the downtown condominium complex housed around an outdoor podium which soon is becoming centre stage of a bizarre pantomime. Screaming and shouting fight to overtake the metal din. Then silence...chh...chh...chh...He's switched to a manual shovel. A visiting Jamaican visualizing bright sun runs out to the balcony still in pajamas. As he tortures his bones on the subzero temperature his sister hurriedly urges him back inside. "Dis is Canada! Dat," she lectures pointing to the blazing orb in the sky, "is jost decoration. It dawsn't doo ehnyting." Cold. Snow. Toronto?

"Take it easy," administered Ayrden's dad, dropping her off.

Uh huh. Recollections of her parents' two hour interview at Ben Gurion security as the contingent sought information on Ayr and her ascendants folded like a Japanese paper duck. Reminiscences of a wrong turn to the Lebanese border. Unpleasant meeting with angry army patrol. The family blocked a single lane dedicated jeep path in position to take fire from beyond the fence, but her dad decided to pause in the moment to snap a photo despite shouts of "Drive! Drive!" from the back seat. Then her mum planned to visit Arab friends in Ramallah, not knowing the terrain or language and appearing very Caucasian in an Israeli-plated rental car. Ayrden baulked, survival sense at last kicking in, and told them to let her know how that turns out. "If I took it any easier I'd be dead," she replied in concurrence with the sudden tension drop from Jerusalem to North America.

"Then don't take it easy," added her mother.

From homey barbarian land to superficial civilization, where everyone wears black and looks anorexic and sun-deprived. But it's funny, society's pervasive misunderstanding of owner-imposed starvation. Oddly enough, experts see ancient saintly self-flagellatory hypo-nourishment as a negative thing, which it would seem it is if the party in question winds up in a box, but what it really stems from is that same stubborn determination that drives the extremist's success coupled with a vision of perfectionist vanity flawed with a fatal ignorance of simple laws of healthy fuel consumption. Not so for the downtown sidewalk joggers or dog people in the park partaking in their weekly soccer game, the play

momentarily arrested as curs Ralph, Gus, and big
Lucy plow through the field in their own amusing
chase. Ayrden scores two goals. "I thought you said
you suck!" proclaimed the strangers who had invited
her to join to even out the numbers. Sam and Lou,
hitherto tied up and left to barking at poignant points
in the match, broke free just in time.

"Are you on our side?" queries an opposing
girl.

Seizing opportunity, Ayrden shiftily replies,
"...Yes."

"No she's not, Jan," corrects the real
teammate. "Watch her, she's tricky."

"They have like five million people on their
team."

"Go yellow man!" Ralph, still smarting from a
ball in the butt, decides to rest his exhausted dog body
behind the goal bags when a mass of people and a ball
in motion storm in his direction and he must scurry
to...

She didn't know who she was anymore. They
didn't need to call her Ayrden, she came all by herself.
Speaking rapidly and flailing arms around aggressively
caused Torontonians to duck not realizing that to
Jerusalemites this was casual discourse, no matter
how intense the tone turned. And the men, who took

her on a date to a smoky bar after she used to jog around her pink desert mountain in the West Bank, who feared relationships when she had been dodging knives, bullets, and bombs, who left an hour long message by knocking the send button of a cellphone crammed into his pocket of him disagreeing with the radio and cursing other drivers on the way to work. Ayrden was used to the Middle Eastern aggression of suitors following her on her walks and conversing while driving backwards in their cars, of religious strangers extolling her breasts and proposing marriage, of inadvertently being taught a set of lyrics unfortunately commencing with "mahmi oh mahmi..." She'd web-hand the lead dog's neck in an instant and shove him into the nearest concrete wall when threats were made or her Russian resemblance harassed since many of those had turned to prostitution. An edging ram into traffic-laden street would do, whatever was available at the time, and she was quick returning shouts of Arabic obscenities to the day workers from the Territories who had been compelled by the mere sight of a girl on the sidewalk to devolve in nature. You see, the extraracial hatred or more correctly the extranational hatred and Israel's lenient democratic justice system made good excuse for a person's innate capacity for criminal violence to select Israeli women and clueless tourists. An Arab preying on his own people would have discovered his swift execution at the hands of the victim's relatives and a complete village cover-up during the subsequent police investigation of his death.

Thus, in accordance with the automatic bag-opening arm motion she'd developed for the weapons search when entering banks, universities, malls, and government offices, and in the same vein the urge not to handle abandoned articles - or if you're a thief, steal them - but more to get out of their estimated explosion radius, she'd resolved that the transience of a person's lifetime required a certain bluntness in communication. To the tease who lounged around her desk acting cutsie she blurted, "Okay, I like you already. Come home with me." He ran out laughing nervously, probably more than a smidgeon frightened at the prospect. Clunk clunk clunk onto the floor fell the jaws of the older men in the office who witnessed the moment in utter disbelief that he was one of theirs. Let's take stock. This was no longer the part of town where cultured refers to soured milks or the presence of old women batting couch cushions half-perched out the window. Where were the washed carpets draping railings and stoned concrete barriers in the vicinity of apartment buildings, the protruding security bars with kids on them hanging precariously above the street, and reinforced steel doors that are paid off in installments? Banks would allow a minus. Mailed articles of value disappear. Another form. One more stamp. A westerner hands over his ticket at the theatre door, whereas the Israeli checks and surrenders his gun.

So, a grand play in order she tried the let's go berserk plan, again. She and her dog got a one way ticket to the desert. They were going to be settlers and reside near open hardy souls. They would live in beauty in a warmer climate. They yearned for sarcastic edgy friendliness. But out of Toronto the airplane veered west...to the desert of British Columbia.

Chapter Eleven

The Middle East turned to disarray as the Middle East tends to do. New regulations had to be set to curb overexertion during heat waves as a regrettable fatality came under scrutiny. Fae offered report, citing that continuous exposed physical exercise in extreme temperatures ruled out fluid replenishment capability. Fact. Given that sedentary countrymen indoors were warned to lap up glasses of water at a rate of one per twenty minutes, non-emergency training put the healthiest young athletes at unnecessary risk. Not exactly was Fae resistant to effects of season change, the recurring sore throat and painfully oilless skin signalling the inauguration of another eight month period devoid of moisture. See that aridity and raise the macho and the consequence will be a vomiting serviceman who denies himself medical treatment, valiantly continuing against his leader's advice. He collapsed from heatstroke and died after days of unsuccessful hospitalization featuring vigorous intravenous therapy and desperate cooling procedures.

Further accidents. Fae was transported up north to where elite heli units dangled men from cables as they all shot through the air too high to believe. A superstitious assortment, fliers. They didn't take remembrance photos lest that's what they become. It's like giving up. Symbols painted on the craft, luck tokens, rituals. The cable had come loose causing its living cargo to plummet into cliffs and sea. Faulty mechanism or human error? She ordered a gear overhaul as recovery dinghies fished out bits of flesh to bury.

As with smoking in the general population, the new country was just starting to see effects of decades of shoddy treatment of its fighters. Puffers were not surprised by their cancers, but what of the illness pervading ex-divers? Naval commandos were a medical glossary in spite of their jock obsession for fitness and nutrition. The port. The port where they dove. The blackened filthy waters off Haifa where the top layer industrial runoff coated head to toe as they climbed out and the floor was a grave of sludge. Blinding underwater conditions simulated Beirut for operations purposes and that was the extent of site research. Fae was scathing. Besides the horrendous neglect of the commandos' health, the practice exhibited disastrously wasteful mismanagement of the navy's human resources. It costs the nation eighteen years to grow a soldier, and so forth, and after a handful of missions normally productive adults were reduced to feeble societal burdens. Who knows? The invalids themselves might have entertained plans for their lives. Not one or two. Tens and tens. Fae sickened. Life's not so great at guiding you onto the right path as much as it is superb at kicking you when you're on the wrong one. Is there a correct direction at all or just nonacceptance?

"What do you want?" entreated her commander, eying her unravelling. A car alarm reverberated high-pitched tones against their frazzled nerves.

"I don't know." She had been on an inhalant for recent asthmatic episodes until the doctor armed with sheets of breathing tests affirmed her lungs better than his. Intellect satisfied, respiratory symptoms miraculously evaporated to make way for incessant stomach cramps which she fed day and night to sop up the acids.

"You'd better get to know and be bothered to fashion a decision." The ringing choked. No, just recharging. "Abstain, and there be plenty out there prepared to decide for you and chances are they do not have your interests in mind and you won't like the outcome." It resumed. "Wait here." He brisked as he exited that room and thrashed about the next, door echoing his slam after the fact. The din quit. An elongated spatula and insulated wire snips crashed to the table just off sight as he reemerged.

"I'm leaving." Israel is aggressive, but it is true anywhere that you will need to fight for who you are, who you want to be, and how you demand to be treated.

The commander menaced opposition to her dangerous defiance.

"I won't stay." Perhaps one is not meant to. Collect existence and go through it. Maybe it is in the impact, the indelible mark which we exchange.

Perpetrators, too, strive for this acknowledgment that they are there, as was Fae's commander under her threat. "You have to learn to stop banging your head against a brick wall."

She understood...how the staff is a serpent... she understood...water equals wine...all is possible... my masters...mankind...are our G-ds and they are but one...the sea and the heaven...water and water over there...a reflecting pool...mystics...in all the potential ...they were not unique...in each being the universe... to exist...continuous formation...unending love...G-d is being...witness of eternity...ruin...she understood. Fae perished.

Chapter Twelve

"Shmaaa Is-ra-el." The grave tone prayer reader on Yuli's clockradio was an early morning terror each day as she awoke, like the very rumblings of G-d, though the station was never switched over. Recalling that the water dreams subsided when she had more or less reconnected with her niece there came now a stark unveiling. Maliya is an island name. And that's precisely where her niece is. Ben, on the other hand, was eying Ofer eying him. As long as he remained in Israel...

"Ben, I'm an idiot, aren't I?" Yuli confessed, figuratively groping for a way out of the corner.

"We weren't going to say anything," he teased, employing the plural to represent himself and the rest of the world.

"No, specifically, how did Maliya come about her name?"

"Etymology? You haven't yet supplied me with the original one. I'm aware I mustn't look for it."

"They'll know."

"By this time everyone knows."

"Besides, I already did."

"Oh yeah," nodding, not having any memory whatsoever of that information transference. "People "will talk of this for years to come. You will be you, and I will be that man who went crazy."

"It's been done. Notwithstanding, you researched Maliya when she and Aram started romancing. What was her occupation in the army?"

"Something unspectacular. Wait. Arts troupe. Hardly dangerous. The only thing they massacred were show tunes, perhaps deservedly. She's a good kid, if not spoiled rotten. Don't forget Maliya was a loner."

"Our loaner."

Back then Maliya and Fae had both entered the army, only one to return. And she was right where she was supposed to be for it was Ofer who chose her by name.

"The couple was desperate to raise that lovely child, in a normal community I might add, despite the lawlessness of the whole episode. Attendance at regular school in the public eye. Even the army training had nothing to do with army, and you can guess who's pull got her in there. His one chance to get a hold of her he didn't use. Ofer remained at arm's length, hands off. No period unaccounted for. Should there be a scheme for her amidst the agent's delusions

"Maliya just is not capable."

"You, more than anyone, suspected her."

"Of course I did. She took my Prime Minister. And there was a mystery surrounding her. My intuition couldn't miss that."

"I fear for them." Yuli's spirit was weighted. Ben couldn't pass on her insight either.

Fae's commander received a directive to activate the program.

"Time for a trip, Yuli. Ofer's on the move."

"Is that wise? How are we to find them? The Hawaiian islands are not 500 kilometre long Israel."

"I believe Aram and Maliya are in the soup even if we don't lead trouble to their doorstep. As for exactly where that is," Ben respired with effort as though the molecules of oxygen, every last one, had been marshalled to a spot under the sofa, "where is anywhere?"

Yuli had thought him on the verge of something profound with the breathing antics. Now that he'd spat out nothing, maybe it still was. "We can't just skip trace and follow the relative trail."

"Because that's you."

"They won't have a phone. Names?"

"Could change from week to week."

"Money?"

"No cards. Ghost transactions overseas. You pay good negative interest for that."

"I can imagine."

"Set up properly in the tropics a person would not have the same need for perpetual financing as in a city or northern country."

"Lose yourself amongst a lot of people, or nobody."

"Or others like you."

"Criminals?"

"Under the table money source. Homemade security. Aversion to outsiders. The kind that couldn't afford to give you away to a stranger brandishing your glossy."

"We search ideas. Available real estate. Where would I go?"

"Not a great time has elapsed, Yuli. Once we whittle down the possibilities of today we should find ourselves in the yard next door."

"I'm underwhelmed by your oversimplification of the immensity of this task. It's well seen the two of you believed you could fix the country single-handedly. I'm torn. Is that being naïve or arrogant?"

"Actually, both," pointing at her correctively.

Several pseudonyms would have come and gone for the number of days Ben and Yuli scanned the islands. Preferable were the aerial views over coasts of smaller land masses, reasonable access yet remote enough. Guides' tales of the chains as havens for locals residing illegally were of interest. Social matters of disputed status, ecological retrieval of endangered areas in the face of commercial aspirations, mere static blots with no governmental teeth fussing to nip the area's old world inhabitants. Could you spell Aram any other way? Not sure of what to seek until it's in front of your face so obvious. "Does that appear familiar to you?"

"Clue number three: traces of the homeland."

"The wind generators surpass what we've got."

"Did they mail order solar power arrays straight from Israel? Hey everybody, I'm here! Come attack me in my environmentally conscientious abode."

"Are we certain it was any more than a stopover?"

"Don't, don't give them ideas. Your head is a gigantic petri dish for the actual."

"Like, how do you stop a distant boat moving across the water?"

"You're that girl, the friend to whom a guy would bring home his new hot lover with the cough only to have you predict she'd die of consumption and by act four she does."

"Awh!" gasping.

Inside the home unmistakably theirs were Aram and Maliya no longer. It had been a plain of battle. Here is Grenade. Ragged. Defiant. Ben and Yuli, seized in the devastation and dread of this bloodied monster clomping through furniture to end also them, faltered defenseless. Then Grenade collapsed. "Huh! Aram and Mal should've finished the job."

"Do you think they escaped?"

"Look at him."

"You are familiar with the saying about the other guy?"

"Where now?" Ben queried of himself.

"Depends on the passports you issued."

"They'll be working off another scheme at this date."

"Something different."

"No man's land..."

"...to the mainland. And after that?"

"Eh."

Yuli snatched Ben's pointing finger triumphantly. They were sharp, however Grenade had led them to a crucial false assumption regarding his injuries. His condition did not result from combat with Aram and the niece, which professional dust-stirrers would have known. Those markings were in the manner of an agent, each bearing signature style, these of the mercenary Green Eyes. It was fact, regardless of interpretation. And there were more. Grenade had ever the commander. His program was active. Aram and Maliya could panic and run as they wished since Fae's commander was on every step, Yuli and Ben without inkling agitated by the spectacle of near-dead Ofer.

Once on the continent and across the border it was a natural progression ascending the coastline on a drive through the North American desert strip. Not only Middle Easterners would find this route palatable, in fact, most convicts anxious to abandon their part-time Vancouver jails get caught precisely at a handful of choice gas stations in the south of the province as major highways tend to funnel traffic through RCMP surveillance points before otherwise splintering off to greater Canadian freedom. "So, my "friend, you decided to road trip it from the secret service?"

Aram lit in fear at the mention of Ofer.

"Oh, he's idling in the parking lot," Ben assured. "Hey, Mal, whoever you are."

"Returning the sentiment."

"Listen, you're not very good at this hiding thing."

"Not always as it seems."

"I mean, when we were on the terrain and saw what we were dealing with, where else would you be?"

"What if our island place was a beacon? What if we left a present?"

"A bomb? Plague?"

"...and knew you were coming."

"Monitor." Ben realized Aram was ready for a face-off.

"All four."

"Four? Myself, of course," counting down.

"Wouldn't have it any other way. Right, Mal, whoever you are?" mimicking Ben's teasing.

"Try me."

"Yuli," gesturing courteously to the aunt who was silenced in emotional flood and unflinching maternal gaze. "Ofer slash his various code names "slash all the glory that is he," seeking him under a small object. "Maybe that's where you get that from," addressing Maliya.

"There's also the operative who staged that beating with Ofer," Aram added.

"Beating of Ofer." Ben was confounded. "Another operative?" he relayed queasily.

"Key word: staged. Shall I unbolt the door?"

"No, no. I'll go. That way I don't have to witness any executions after I'm done."

In their time they filled the space. Aram, Maliya, Yuli, Ben, Ofer, Green Eyes, the commander. Tense and expectant, watching in soundless communication. Yuli cut the thick emptiness first, impelled by the terrible change overtaking Maliya as she confronted her commander, calling out to her in a whisper, "Fae! Fae!" It was all the voice she had.

Tal's girl partially softened, strangely embraced in the strength of this name which had died.

Long-held suspicion abruptly whacked Aram.

Ofer calculated, livid Maliya was exposed.

Ben whipped toward Yuli, wide-mouthed, for aside from the niece bit he had gained a glimmer of who Fae really was. She was tied to this operative, Ofer's operative. Company be damned. It was a cover. But she is still their family, says Yuli. Yuli only.

They waited. Yuli was ready again. She fixated on Green Eyes, steady brow cautioning him to relax his grip on her beloved niece using their cool friendship with all she could, understanding he betrayed her. Four.

In repeat method Ben gaped at Yuli, joined by Aram and Ofer equally astonished by their mutual recognition. Yuli had dealt with the devil from opposing side. Everyone stopped short.

Chapter Thirteen

"You know spring is tick season."

Her mind wandered away to the rounded sandy hills, intense sun in the valley, the rush of wind through the vast canyon of river, a never ending train snaking alongside it down below. Ayr tuned out the catalogue of vermin and perils and sipped her mug of choco.

"But you only have to worry if you start feeling tingly or dizzy. Pchh. Just ten percent carry Lyme."

Interesting options in vocabulary conservation. Hebrew claims one tenth the number of words found in the English language, of course it is written backwards, without short vowels, and excluding the present tense of the verb "to be".

"It'll take a few black widow bites to put you in the hospital. They're pretty small here."

You get multipersonalitied nouns like "service" running the gamut from restaurant or national service to meaning a large taxi, or in its plural form, washrooms. Explains a lot.

"Our son collects rattlesnakes from this culvert."

Are diamonds or checkers benign?

"Coyotes are the ones making that yip yip yip eee sound. They've been known to carry away cats, and small dogs. Speaking of which...hawks."

Too bad the Israeli hand sign for "just a moment" was not universal. Ayr could touch her fingertips together and with upward turned palm elevate them slightly skyward all day and this noise would somehow still continue.

"Mmm, a cougar will only attack you if he's old, sick, or really hungry."

It wasn't the treacherous Judean Hills but a suicidal soul could still find employment if very enterprising, like licking the arsenic-treated posts of his code-complying entrance stairs whose uneven rises seemed okay to people who tread carefully noticing they were homemade, but that might explain why the dogs keep falling. And there are the billboards in the interior plastered alternately with pictures of grizzlies and packs of coyotes cautioning in big block letters:

DON'T GET STUCK HERE

As if being stranded is ever a conscious decision. Or the fact that settlements are often so far apart that your burning mobile will become grazing feed before the fire department arrives so their policy simply is not to bother. However, abound friendliness and boredom, a lethal combination for the isolationist. Everyone notes your home improvement attempts and one by one a neighbour approaches with curiosity, suggestions, and a better tool. And you know when they go away that they're still watching, wondering why with all the newfangled gadgets available that your method is so pedestrian.

But unabashed curiosity can be a good thing in other areas of human relations, such as when you invite your flirtatious contractor to socialize in a non-job-related appointment, and he doesn't understand. And you receive yet another off-work call, ask him when he's coming to visit, and he still doesn't get it. Now, in Israel, L.A. or any one of the girls at the yeshiva listening to these conversations like some kind of torture would have seized the opportunity to grab the phone and convey something akin to, oh, say, "Ayrden wants you to come over and play. Can you make it here around seven?" but she was left using more cryptic devices, breaking her teeth on consonants.

Clearing his schedule he replies, "In that case I'll fit you in."

They do weddings this way too. Actually, the

pictorial response occurred to her only after hanging up.

Too much spare time and a penchant for science can have strange side effects. You may catch yourself doodling curves of estimated medicinal strength versus time of the commercial yeast infection treatments for differing lengths of days. You might perk up your head and turn synchronously with the herding dogs to investigate a passing car, or whinny. "After you've lived on the Thompson River long enough you'll be feuding with your neighbour over a six-year-old load of gravel."

The place really was quite Jerusalemish, except for the water, the killing, and no one understands you when you speak Hebrew. Both had their unscrupulous realtor types, you know, the kind to whom you'd give a piece of your mind if you thought you could spare it. In Israel it was the owner who improvised a listing extension in lieu of the original floorless laundry-hanging space and leaned out the window, arms doing an airplane guider impression toward the street but without the glowing wands. "You can get a permit to build way over to there," he promised, his fantasy salon completely obliterating the sidewalk. Likewise, Canadians tried to sell plots containing the national highway, parched land where the closest water supply was six hundred feet underground, and lots in the valley beside two main rail lines...but the trains only ran at night. And it's not as if on that cross country route there'd be a lot of them. Or that they had big loud horns or anything like that.

A breathing man walked by.

"Ting."

"Shh. I'm working on it," she muttered in the direction of her abdomen. That was her egg timer. And imaginary triangles are why Ayrden doesn't drink.

Another boring day in British Columbia, as long as the roads are rock slide free and the house isn't blown away by wind. Boring is good. Stay out of the brush. Reasons for having returned? More so for staying so long. Explanations that Israeli tomatoes are identical and tasteless because she personally had picked and passed them green through a prescribed guide hole in a wooden slat. Memories of the haunted cop giving her a lift against regulations because there she appeared like a ghost on that very spot where the previous week another girl had been before being murdered. They believed even tourists were returning souls. They bet shaking her family tree would drop a Jew out of somewhere. Recriminating prediction of a venture farther east. Admission of the family doctor in regard to Ayr's old adoration for her no good ex, "It made me sick!"

She had met the one in question just off the pay phone with news of upcoming basic training. He said, "Chma..." She should've gone to the army. "Chma." A Sephardi. It's like a rule.

As a present given an empty book. "Then again, what would you do with money?"

COUNTERPOINT

<u>Counterpoint</u>

book 3

Chapter One

"What is this place?" Ofer rumbles.

"Right here, where your feet stand," the commander snaps back.

Blackened outlines of men they were as the aspect panned from head-on abaft. Not so much a hue, more, erased. And their diminutive figures framed introduction to an immensity of cleft, boulder gorge, waterfall, seemingly swallowing them in comparison to a mere single point.

Aram offers, "Buddhists consider the location their spiritual world centre."

"Thank-you for the clarification," Ben returns with corrosive satisfaction.

"You always had it."

"And what position precisely would that be on a map?" interrogates the commander.

Yuli interferes, "It makes a difference?"

"You have to be where you are," states Maliya in tow.

"About this far into no-man's-land one starts to contrive a murder-suicide pact," Ofer reminds the commander of their mission.

"And we're back," he responds.

"I've got a locale. They're up Deadman River," solves the technician inducing quizzical looks from a computer scientist. "What? Not on top of religions' hot spots? You've got your main ones, and they're quite specific."

Yuli grows impatient. "Couldn't all of us just enjoy one moment of completeness without you dredging up the volumes of our past fragmenting unpleasantness?"

"Now who's using the pronouns?" Ofer threatens.

"Present. Dire predicament of the present," Ben corrects anxiously.

"There you go again," Yuli crosses off another philosophical error.

Aram whispers to Ben a secret, "No one really understands the concept of time."

"Feeling bound by it, but necessarily so?" Maliya confirms.

Aram consults with her, "Thus arises the question of linearity."

"It's in question?" the commander inquires.

"Of course," Ayrden comments in overtone.

"Have you noticed the company we keep?" frets Ben. He briefly closes his eyes. Upon opening, "No. They're still here."

"So much for 'I am the universe'," Maliya tuts.

Aghast was the team of surveillants. "Unbelievable."

"Then why bother with a discussion?" Ayrden cuts as headphones are removed.

"Who that was!"

"For some reason which never fails to flabbergast, Israelis are under the impression that when speaking Hebrew they morph into another plane invisible and inaudible to all foreigners. I can't tell of the times I hijacked private conversations being the only one around for miles. Terrified expressions, honestly. If I was literate in their tongue, what next?"

"The assassinated Israeli Prime Minister!"

"Not to mention one murky secret serviceman who did him in."

"How do they let these people into the country?" processes the engineer.

Ayrden shrugs and complains, "I ripened two years on a security roster shelf before my own army trusted me."

"Trusted?"

"We still don't," a host of machinery issues forth, voiced by the ensconced technician.

"Translate that!"

"Enough excitement for you, Comp-Sci." Tech continues to Ayrden, "Seriously, your Semitic friends were polled. Even they thought you were a spy."

"Really? Jokesters. How goes it in the sun?" she reminisces. "Oh yeah," reconvening.

Ofer and Green Eyes pounded walls with focused severity. "Supporting or not?"

"They're looking for us," the Canadians advise.

"If you knock this down there'd be a nice spread here," Ofer fashions.

"Yes, let's redecorate," suggests Ben.

Aram slumps a great pot to the table, its ample volume yet simmering.

"Ah, now the soup's arrived. Perfect," Ben can't resist, "need that dose of dioxin. Or perhaps you're a polonium-210 guy? Myself, I'm a sucker for ye olde poison letter. What can I say?"

Yuli drops the wallet recently pickpocketed

and in which she was currently snooping plumb to the floor.

"It's more a stew."

"Maliya?" her uncle assumes.

"Maliya can't cook coffee," Aram clarifies.

"Bet she has a to-die-for tea," steeps Ben.

"Nobody ever asks more than once," she wonders.

Ofer grunts to her clever ploy, nodding.

"What I could have learnt from my niece," Yuli agrees.

"And you are supposed to be somewhat but not somewhat her uncle," remarks Aram at Ofer's unfamiliarity.

"One could say the same of you."

"Easy. Flashing red light and siren. I'll try the nut, onion, and soy rice," tempts Ben. "Umm. A POW would hand over his PM to sup such a feast."

Ofer replies, "I'd give 'im away in peacetime. You can keep your bowl o' rice."

"Don't be afraid," Ben mocks.

"Discipline."

Green Eyes lectures, "Discipline is not in the extreme, but in moderation. There is a place between austerity and gluttony where soul and body coexist to their mutual benefit."

"Come on, Ofe. Be a happy little medium."
Ben chokes, "Commander, Eyehole, whatever you are
called, you don't look so good."

Ofer broods, "Aide, you should never have
dinner with the secret service."

"Did you shift Shamir from the ballot to the
plate?"

"Main course: chicken," Aram proudly
declares.

"That doesn't sound boiled," Maliya shows
off.

Listening to her, Ben heeds Ofer's warning,
"I'll pass."

Yuli tastes the rotten dish, gagging, "Ugh!"
only to gather herself and go in again in the hope of a
more favorable response. "Phhe!" finally spitting the
vile morsels out.

Ben questions her methodology, "What's the
matter, optimist? Not disgusting enough the first
time?" Next, turning to Aram, "This is it? Your sole
means of defence is salmonella?"

"That was unintentional," he swears.

"So this is why you're so thin!" proclaims
Yuli, attempting to cleanse her palate with air.

"Have you had the custard pie?"

"I regarded it as meat!"

Maliya accepts, "We, too, are averse to overindulging in animal."

"Are you delicious?" Yuli stakes out the pie.

"No. No I am not!" rescues Ben.

"Would you like some?" Maliya entertains.

"Oh, I don't need any. Maybe just a bite. Are you going to? Well then alright, and a cup of tea, dear."

"He killed another leader?" the forces are edgy.

"Fresh dill. They share the name," Ayrden enlightens the engineer. "I know."

"You do know," convinced.

She hangs her head, "I don't know. I just ceased asking questions."

Keenly responsive, "They're blocking our feed...dampening us with static."

"They're listening to the radio," Tech restores calm. "In the vast wasteland of the interior it's difficult to tune in. The only station for miles is..."

"Don't put on CBC! No one can be that cruel."

"And the topic...politics of yard sales."

Groans.

"Stop talking. Stop talking. Just play a song."

"Bach or Kookshow?"

"I don't have enough coffee for this."

"Oh, that bird is back again," Comp-Sci charges.

Nerves fray. "What would you like me to do about it?"

"I was actually thinking of installing a complaints box," Ayrden tends, much to their intrigue, "which I will never open."

"Very military," the geeks commend.

To that comment she simulates placing a note in the fanciful receptacle.

The engineer folds his own nonexistent memo, inserting it into said box now marvelously having crossed the space and conveniently been set beside him. "You mistook and slighted our compliment."

"Don't get me started," Ayr reproves.

He removes his paper under her glare.

"To be alive, sleep-deprived, and bad tempered. We may have just solved the enigma of the Israeli disposition."

Tech dissertates, "But the country is quite tolerant of other religions in its midst."

"Bahai? Yes. Keep Christianity to yourself. That's touchy."

"Non bloodthirsty ones."

"Complaint box!"

"Aram, how does a person increase his likelihood of dying prematurely?"

Maliya, Yuli, he, and Ben mind Grenade with concern.

"Be the Prime Minister of Israel and engage in the peace process."

"You comedian, you," Ben backhandedly flatters Ofer. "There are no legislative moguls here."

"Full of yourselves. This group is nothing now. I was remarking on the current one in a coma."

Faces awaken.

"Of that I was skeptical," the aide points at Ofer's nose as if winning a wager.

"Ben?" Yuli cautions.

"However, if the one addressed insists he poses a problem..."

Maliya steps between her two uncles, "If you persist meditating on this infernal theme it'll be my honored duty to give hit with a stick!"

"Strictly inspirational," derides Ben.

"Right," Maliya recites unconvincingly.

"Such passion. It's disappointing you'd take no pleasure," Ofer goads.

Green Eyes reviews Hindu philosophy for her benefit, "Passionate is the warrior."

"And Maliya contemplates in the manner of a priest?" Ofer investigates.

"No patience," she confesses. "The only thing I reflect upon is myself in the mirror."

Her commander smirks.

Yuli is riled at his glibness, for lack of understanding. "You!" opposing him.

"Concise yet effective," majority rules.

"'Upon resting my eyes I saw myself learning the ten secrets of the universe...'" Yuli apes Green Eyes' faked depth with disdain.

"...from a translucent filmstrip projected by angels..." Maliya interrupts, picking up on the impression familiar to her.

"...under a waterfall," the two women complete in unison.

Yuli realizes, "That was you?"

"In my vision," pausing to emphasize authorship, "the spirits ascended and descended alongside the cascade."

"Well done, Mal," Aram supports.

Ben is dubious, "And what were they, the secrets of life?"

"I can eat bread. That's all I got."

Aram interprets, "Penetrating arbitrary social conditioning, assumed boundaries."

"It's entirely clear now," Ben nevertheless unconverted.

"You can also wage war," deciphers Yuli.

Ofer and his subordinate close ranks, "We're being monitored."

"The hawk's incessant squawking."

Muted, "I could've assured it be vulture."

"Oh, just strike the feathered beast with two stones!" blurts Ben.

Expounding, "Canadians routinely check license plates, fly over the back country with scanners. It was only a question of time."

Aram and Maliya witness Ofer's tutelage, momentarily content.

"Police? Army?" the aide straggles for reinforcements.

"What army?" Israeli secret service cajole.

"What army?!" Canuck scientists echo.

Chapter Two

"We've heard some interesting tales about you," the engineer pokes.

Ayrden catches the room chatter interspersed with her eavesdropping duties. "Are you certain it was me?" humbled.

"Travels to Israel." Polygraphs would have that rated as the cold or control statement acting as a lead-in.

"Among other things," somewhat unresponsively.

"Ever in Jordan?" raising the thermostat.

"Apparently," glimpsing, aware of the top international news headlines of the year.

"There was a siting." Here it comes. "Recognize anything in particular?" Transplanted, hovering over Ayr's station, the engineer presented her with a photograph of one Maliya under watch...

Not a flinch, although now attentive.

...as well as a representation of the very passport in her own name.

"Yeah? Nice picture of my documentation," densely. "That was from when I was in..."

The engineer fingered a connection between Ayr's I.D. and Maliya.

"...Israel," comprehending. "No!"

"You said you knew about Jordan," finding fault in the flow of her argument.

"I was kidding. Current events."

"We pegged you for their spy."

Comp-Sci and Tech peek at each other, "I thought she was our spy."

"You think she's our spy?"

Ayrden, intense, "And she is me?"

"That goes without saying."

"Unless you're Ayrden," Tech taunts, "in which case you'll require the movie version detailing how it happened from start to finish."

Overhearing, "How...?"

"Customs control had you recently reentering the country. Naturally, you were already here..."

"You know you're not really here," again, Tech.

"...in the armed forces, having returned the requisite number of years ago..."

Ayr performs a double flat-hand slam on the table, "Why are you talking so slowly?"

"...so as not to be a National Security Outcast."

Comp-Sci seeks the obligatory piece of information, "Why did you go to Israel, anyway?"

"When my family related heroic legends of our cave-dwelling ancestors, literate skirt-wearing barbarians and of guttural tongue, I assumed we were Jewish."

"Sounds reasonable."

"Hey, remember the time you were going to quit your business, put your stuff in storage, and go volunteer in the third world?" rally the guys amongst themselves.

Laughter.

"You should do that," soberly intimates Comp-Sci.

Ayrden fixes on him.

The engineer churned out the remaining pictures.

"They're Israeli. These are our voices," she determines.

Opted the gents for further study.

Engineering a denial of their motion, "In testing, Ayr labelled nationals who didn't speak at all. There was a man who said one word, and it was in English."

"With an accent?" Tech displays his cosmopolitan savvy.

"He said, 'Hi.'"

An interval.

Comp-Sci takes the torch, "No dialect?"

"Say it," orders the engineer.

"Hi," complying begrudgingly with a regrettable realization the flame was gone.

"Like that."

Deflated, Comp-Sci imitates the complaints procedure.

Tech next.

Then underestimated Ayrden.

Not to omit the annoyed engineer.

"Aha!" triumphs Aram.

"What do you mean, 'Aha!'?" Maliya counters. "You are completely wrong."

"Are you two on the verge of entering another fascinating Far Eastern ethical dilemma while we're still queasy from your repast?" marvels Ben.

Yuli shushes him.

Emerald Eyes is stirred, "Expand."

Ofer gets drawn in as audience to a farce much too subtle that would his practical impulses embrace.

"Why would someone's near-death experience contain favourite teachers who have passed on? Must not distant acquaintances have their own 'heaven' if you will with loved ones and relatives who are close to them, there?"

"That argument infers a there and a here, also in a heaven which is a physical unknown."

"If you will," mediates Ben.

"The discrete spaces are solely reference to a person's limited perception..."

"I can't begin to dissect what's wrong with that," Aram debates.

"Let me finish," rebukes Maliya good-naturedly. "...of his surroundings."

"Doable."

"I propose that by extrapolating from the basic idea of a hologram or gene set..."

"Ben, quiet."

"Ah, preemptive."

Demeanors judged Yuli.

"She was right," the aide pronounces. "I was extrapolating from the basic idea of a hologram or gene set just this morning."

"...people take with them pieces of others' energy, pieces obviously replaceable to the donors..."

"Holey aunt of Frankenstein."

"...which then are recreated in death as entire beings just as they had been encountered in life."

Aram concedes, "That was profound."

"That is to say, not recreating actual physical bodies but the energy essence of a person. A spirit."

"Your conception could parallel and be the reason behind psychological influences among the living: actual energy transfer."

"Or, not transfer as much as alteration."

Ben commentates, "Tisn't a freak storm. This is what they do."

Yuli upstaging, "Thus to be in many places at once, leaving your stamp through accomplishments and personal impressions."

"For a positive outcome..."

Ofer joins the symposium after Aram's turn, "...or a very bleak one."

"Teaching, healing. To affect by mere proximity instead of tremendous concrete demonstrations."

Green Eyes won't be outdone by his consort, "Shake off the bad energy of villains who plague the innocent with their own burdens."

"Okay. New subject: Weather. Good or bad?"

Aram ignores Ben, "By your definition here and there are indistinct since Yuli as creator can be in both."

"Agreed, although creation is a problem."

"Interaction. And part of a wavelength is itself the wavelength."

"Totally."

"So tending a small garden with wholeness leaves an indelible imprint on the rest of the world, not just a metaphor."

"You do win," mesmerized he turned her contradictory argument around to suit his theory.

"Enough! Even Ben here," indicating himself, "fully got that everyone wins, inclusive of these two who'll no doubt conduct interesting experiments for all sorts of nefarious purposes, if they haven't done so already."

"Be careful of the company you keep," one gives notice.

"It heeds."

"Are they talking in code?" the engineer requests definitively from Ayrden.

"Yes and no. Not in the literal sense, but they are discussing their fate."

"Obvious enemy types gathered together half a planet from their origin, not killing each other, eating."

Comp-Sci also at a loss, "They opted for a brain blowout?"

"Perhaps it's a decoy," distrusts Tech.

"What are they plotting in Canada?"

"Unclear."

"The transcriber is malfunctioning," Tech essays to adjust a fictitious knob on Ayr.

"Isn't Ayrden supposed to understand them, that being the reason why she's here?"

"Allowing that an Israeli operative wasn't posing as me none of us would be," searching for credit.

Alas the engineer collapses her pride, "Recruiting did uncover that letter to the CIA."

"Told you there had to be one," as Tech and Comp-Sci exchange cash.

"American green. That's like," counting, "a million dollars Canadian."

"Neither of you should cross into the States any time soon."

Refocusing on said correspondence, "Crazy, huh?"

"If I recall, a CV with blot-outs, a stated preference for vegetables, rambling, begging access to natural light and outside air sufficiently supplied by a cracked window, and confusion as to the intent behind sending the letter in the first place somewhere in the vegetables."

"Beauty."

"You owe me another twenty."

"Peculiarities of that approach aside, the job

"market is tough to crack. Appreciate that when I called placement companies in the field of physics/ engineering there would always be a secretary who didn't grasp their common ground. One replied that for an engineer a physics position was, and I quote, 'a whole other world'. Tell that to U. of T. engineering students sauntering each morning into the physics building just over the street for classes."

"I'm not getting the gist."

"It's the same world!" Turning from the guys to Ayr in earnest, "Why do you change your name every three and a half years?"

Chapter Three

"Shoot something!"

"You can't set up video streaming like that," Comp-Sci comments on the technical glitch they are undergoing.

Tech objects, "But this is the way my system works."

"It doesn't," the engineer states bluntly.

"Maybe if you disconnect the external drivers."

"They're the computers' drugs," Ayrden sympathizes. "Not the FireWire hub! I'm on that, too."

"Would it help to switch all cables over to USB?" Tech offers.

The engineer rejects, "Envisage a bigger traffic jam."

Typing madly, Comp-Sci explores internal processes, "OS-DOS? That's no good. Let's get Bill Gates out of the Mac. Just a minute...We're restored."

"Solved?" the engineer assents. "Our functions were crossed?"

"Here, Tech, touch this. It's safe. I," emphasized, "know what I'm doing."

"Game," following instructions. Rapidly his

hair spans out like a poor blow-dry, rising in every direction, defying gravity.

Comp-Sci captions, "No, mum, I didn't skip school and go to the science centre and play with that big electrostatic ball."

"Touché. We can say that in Canada without requiring Teletype."

"Israelis employing their second official language compel bleeps."

"Read this for me then," Comp-Sci passes a random document to Tech.

"Date de registre." Successively pronouncing it anglicized, "Date de register. What's so difficult about that?"

"Must be I don't wear glasses."

"This is your driver's license, and in it you're wearing glasses."

"Under the conditions, though, it's not necessary I use them."

"You would imagine that if somebody approached for their license photo with the aid of lenses they'd be legally required to wear them." He reconvenes with the screen realizing that rendering the images for viewing will take time, "By all means, 'Prepare the video for display'."

"There was a guy who envisioned himself

"flying passenger planes, only he couldn't discriminate between red and green," recollects Ayrden.

"How open-minded of him," esteems the engineer, "as hundreds of trusting vacationers plummet from the sky to their horrific deaths."

"The fact that he wasn't allowed to drive a car should've been the giveaway."

The computer speaks, "During the last five seconds prior to proceeding, the status area will display a countdown from five to zero and sound five beeps to let you know your time to abort is nearly up, the last beep being longer and lower in pitch. Bip. Bip. Bip. Bip. Beep."

"Secondary transmissions. Module one off line."

"Aw, secondary transmissions..."

"Bleep!" Ayr rescribes.

Furious Grenade challenges his subcommand, "Hold me back, because I'm going to kill him. I'm gonna burn down his house!"

"Why not just shave my back, hand me my club, and we'll call it a day?" spurs Aram, contempt layering condescension.

"Do you want my opinion?" Maliya

interposes rhetorically.

Apprehensive of further incident, Yuli and Ben mumble, "No."

"This garden doesn't invite any more fertilizing today."

Ben appends, "But thank-you for your thoughtfulness at any rate."

"Fathom orbiting Earth and observing the passing of sunset after sunset in one 24-hour period, Aram. Ninety minute flight around the world."

He migrates to meet her in that mode, "What about the twin paradox? Space travel approximating the speed of light slows clocks, and so, aging."

"It's a quick circuit, however, ordinary astronauts falling with gravity in our circumference aren't nearly that fast."

"Superman's time reversal episode, soaring against and unwinding the Earth's spins?"

"I never got that."

"You're using cartoons in this debate?" marvels Ben.

"Relativity is perplexing," Maliya renews. "Individual frames of reference, there needs to be a common truth."

"Like no fiction," the aide still kicking.

"There is. We are deluded by what we see.

"Look beyond."

"Is the astronaut younger, truly? Man's body is suited to our gravity, a lack of weight-bearing exercise deteriorating bone mass much more expeditiously than old women's menopause causing tremendous damage during their short time in space. I am resolved that on a mortal level it evens out either way. Does science really expect to cheat life?"

"Time and space are meaningless," maintains Aram. "At light speed they infinitely compress."

"Pure massless energy."

"Hey, do you think we bind our spirit to our mass with gravity?"

"Of course it's serious," Ben, sincerely flabbergasted.

"Atmospheric soul?"

"Cool. Gravity and electromagnetism to me are similar language. Both promote uniform circular motion. Neutral matter's net zero charge in gravity is perceivable as having charge and field with respect to electromagnetism."

"Cold and hot," she summarizes. "Gadi and Tal would laugh me out of the room, but I couldn't escape..."

On cue, "Funny, neither could Gadi and Tal."

"...paralleling solar-planetary structure and

"atoms."

"Cold and hot," Aram validates. "Huge and slow versus miniscule electrons exhibiting a velocity fractions off the speed of light. Aside from the obvious differences it's logical."

"Extreme velocity and all its rule-breakers are more readily achievable on the smaller scale. Perhaps the soul is of said scale and thus, too, is freed from classical limitations."

Yuli is touched the family recombined into a single sentence, "Gadi and Tal wouldn't have laughed you out of the room."

"In spite of your shoddy physics."

Comp-Sci bent over under his station and fiddled with a precisely arranged floor-based paperwork tower for which he was accountable.

"Filing?"

He peruses a report given to his collection, "This is how you perform write-ups? Three choices of numbers in the address, a zip code the place is near, and a map with an arrow. It's as if you just don't care anymore."

"As if. Say, they're erecting a glass fence come netting contraption, absurdly costly monstrosity of an eyesore, around a Torontonian bridge since too "many pedestrians are using it to commit suicide. See?" Tech has got a schematic for display.

"That looks really...impressive," Comp-Sci smirks.

"Then how do you stop jumpers from doing themselves in?" he polls.

Ayrden tenders, "Raise minimum wage."

"You're awfully snooty for someone who spent last season running from a little wind and rain."

"It's called a typhoon."

"Semantics. At least the authorities..."

"Meaning, us," garbles Comp-Sci.

"...didn't have to lower a river to save me."

"I can still function in society," Ayr declares, "I just choose not to."

"You're in the right place then."

The engineer, adept representing himself as stern and displeased, "Were you going to inform me about this or must I wait for it to appear on the news?"

"Sleeper-cell chatter is up," Comp-Sci spills. "Local."

Ayr jumbles her realities, "Our watch list is retaining those ones? On the airwaves they're cleared, cleaned, and pressed into suits of purity and innocence, picture-perfect immigrants."

"Serves them right," orates Tech, "uprooting from that third world hellhole on an arduous journey to improve their lives in a decent civilized country through menial jobs, sweat, and determination."

"Yeah, I don't buy it either."

"Why doesn't the entire Middle East leave there and come and play out its battles exactly here in Canada?"

"Reconnaissance," the engineer resolves.

"Who's team has that detail?"

"Sucker sandwich, double-flanked."

"Us, we're the team. We're the only team, hence, our detail. Stop flaring your nostrils at me."

Ben engages in pseudo psychoanalytical discourse in kind, "Strike answer to the bottomless question and you will sense chills discerning endless more in every direction, too many to set in phrase."

"Yet somehow you do," measures Yuli.

"I was absolved meeting the owner once I beheld her garden. My condolences, proprietress. If convinced it would be of remedy, I'd pee on the blasted grass myself."

Growing impatient she goes to smack his waving magician arms, "Precisely who are you trying to impress?"

"Don't think yourself into a box," Maliya steers.

"Yes, don't," Grenade seconds...altogether alternate interpretation, although along those lines, "Find something to eat," he causes Green Eyes to exit.

"Happy Yom Kippur." The Goth brothers' take on food would assuredly be an imprudent bite.

Retaliating, Grenade's view targets Ben to the point it assumes almost physical touch, "It doesn't get any fresher than alive."

Chapter Four

"They confiscated my communications clip at the airport," Ayrden apprises as her backlit colleagues reassemble in the hush of sandy-hilled darkness.

The engineer scolds, "You didn't bury it outside as instructed?"

"Can't we get waived, being a counterterrorism unit...and a countercounterterrorism unit?"

"That's back to terrorism again, not us opposing rival factions of an insurgent nature," as he speaks Comp-Sci, too, submerges into the mire of his predecessor's confusion, "and in so doing protecting Canadian peace and security on home soil and all that."

"Nice quote."

"With any luck they'll get each other," the engineer's pragmatic cynicism voices.

"Ah, how white man remains on top by keeping minorities feeling downtrodden so as to fight amongst themselves and bother the women."

Comp-Sci, roused, "Do they know about each other?"

"Let's hope not."

"Hope's a good policy for the country's last

"line of defense," Ayr conveys.

"Which, again, is just us," replays Tech.

"It's sufficient," the engineer somewhat assures as he establishes the intriguing mechanism that was to be their set of wheels.

"Enough scratches? We can rely on this antiquity to work?"

"The car's okay. I need her to run, not prance around emaciated and date rock stars."

Further bewilderment, "That's a car?"

The gawkers continue, "Tank. Jeep, maybe."

"When there's a stand specifically to support your common household machine-gun-on-the-fly it's not a car," Ayr defines.

"Also, wrong plates," points out Comp-Sci.

"I have to change registration because of cross-country travel?" feigning ignorance. "What a boon for serial killers," the engineer probes into vehicle cavities most deftly hidden.

Tech launching on fanciful wing of conspiracy, "...and our girl's alias of the week."

"Stocked with supplies, rangers as agency. How else were we to perform functions without a bloomin' bill in parliament or judge's insignia?"

"In secret." Got it.

"By plane Ayrden couldn't smuggle a com

"clip. We're still short that piece," his curt sullenness permeating their ride as they motored ahead. "Map."

Handy Tech complied and assumed the task of navigator as the engineer provided direction.

"Off road. Not quite, there's a dirt path. It may be marked."

"The skyway?"

"Skyway?"

"Skyway?!" Ayr and Comp-Sci unhinged.

"Good. It is marked," minding the driving, rather delighted the mission was advancing satisfactorily.

"What ever happened to the ground way?"

The engineer swerved upward, headlights grabbing the side of a precipice, "Relax. Don't spend your last few moments worrying."

Tech coincides, "Climbing isn't nearly as precarious as...descent!"

"Brakes!"

"Brakes!"

Vainly jamming his foot into the passenger side metal floor, "You do have them on this thing? This is what they're for!"

They finally halted when the road quit, situating them at the base where was stationed an exaggeratedly hermetic expanse of a ranch. Ride unspoken, the four donned night visors and entered the log structure in quiet shadow.

Contacting a lower cupboard door in search of the narrow ingress...

"Where have you been?" asks the box of the engineer in officious pitch while rooms brighten suddenly and unannounced.

Affording the luxury of deep breath, "A post office?" the three synchronize.

"Yes and no," intones the attendant delivering a letter.

"I got into Trent!"

"We'll abide until dawn, require a fill, but will take other means," the engineer whips out his government debt trace card.

Successful interaction with the depot's machine. "Yey!" harmonizes the trio.

"Do you want me to do anything else?"

Chest knocking from their trip which soon will proceed by other means than a trusted deathtrap, "Can you fix my health?" Comp-Sci braves at last.

Ben contemplates the commander's fare, "Now I know why we don't have mice this year, honey. We're in for a bunch of snakes."

"Back people into a corner and they get

"desperate, at which point it makes no difference whether they are ultimately good or evil. They're desperate and you are in front of them," rationalizes Aram. "To take responsibility for your arrival at that final confrontation, even if right then morality is with you and what has to be done is obvious, perhaps having made better choices it wouldn't have turned this way at all."

"I'll cut you out so fast you'll miss the scissors flying past your nose for the cord," Grenade neglects his own blanching for another stab at Ben.

"Oh, give self-serving schemes of world contortion a rest."

Aram coheres to his thesis, "Should I conquer in the end I also will suffer. Thus, I shall lose."

"They live in a culture of fear, rendering their perspective conservative, protectionist. Not a premise from which to base clear-minded decisions," Ayrden elucidates the Israeli situation for the North Americans.

"A lovely people," settles Tech.

"When I splintered the wen-do board I shattered eighteen years of society's brainwashing that women are weak and should live in constant "anxiety," Maliya confesses. "It's popular culture. But since reflection is the order of the day, males dictating the status of women be so displays that it is they who are insecure. Characters attract those like themselves."

"What did I do to deserve this?" Aram terms the sum of their notions in double entendre.

"Perhaps you are manufacturing a diversion from your life to delay resolving and engaging with your truth. Now or later..."

"Power games. Aggression," lists Ayrden, "Hot air."

"You're describing a country whose manual I've never read, and Israel's I did," Tech is disillusioned with the military publishers. "I surmise then the Palestinians are not 'undaunted by Israeli military strength'? Line five."

"Depressed and self-destructive, hopelessly sabotaging their future. Same action, different motivation."

Maliya reaches pivotal point, "The will to move toward a source of hope."

"Stop already," Ben tires of her preaching. "Everybody knows who you are."

"I see you, Fae," Yuli softly rasps before clearing throat with cough.

Ben was stuck on the coarse grinding sound for an instant. Or two.

"Do you?" Green Eyes evaluates, "Do you perceive her many faces?"

"I am as you look at me."

"Whoa there, White Buffalo Calf Woman. I read this story."

"Ben?"

"Revere the spirit as aggregate of multiple lives and receive favour, or behave like an amorous cowboy..."

Aram interposes, "A Native hunter."

"...and...Poof!...to your detriment."

"Umm, tastes like chicken," salivates Ofer.

"Better," alludes Green Eyes to the earlier model.

"Um."

"Here. Try this."

"Um," endorsing the charred bit.

"A tangy side dish could be had on the cheap vegetable rack if you volley into town and lob off the vying senior citizens," Aram serves.

"Or," Ben aids, "word is it can be a sweet deal adopting one of those 'people' if you're a trifle "hungry and in want of a bath. Get a choice one, I hear there may be a country home in it for you and mat by the fire."

"Do they even like people?"

"I vote no, a multitude of murders kind o' reinforcing the hunch."

Then it was again the turn of Gruesome Duo, "I expect he'll have sense enough to save himself and chew on Aram's rotting carcass until someone discovers."

"He won't miss that arm."

"Seen it before."

Ben hails Ofer's breadth, "My, you have all the fun."

"And I get in all the trouble," Aram recounts.

"Time for a walk."

"This is the country," Aram informs Ofer. "In lightning the best-looking ground in an open flat field is a two metre tall pole of water."

Ben demonstrates, "K-chhh!" arcing his discharging hand into Aram.

"Wilder curs can hold their own against predators such as coyotes which recognize keen survival instincts, unlike weak overbred prissies with their DVD movies, hot running water, central heating, and cheap vegetable rack." He left.

Speechless.
"Did he just reckon lightning is a coyote?"
"He got the canine analogy."
Speechless.

Chapter Five

"I do that," Ayrden volunteers. "The brake oil is in two little thingies and the engine oil is in that thingamajiggy."

"And if the all wheel drive demands a parallel park add another two hours."

Comp-Sci is in a clutter, "Does anyone else need to do laundry?"

"We just got here."

"You might be some of those really lazy people that pack a backpack full of dirty attire," tugging at one poignantly gamy article of underclothing.

"Oh!" they roar in unison, "Keep it a mystery," the slogan of basic training when togetherness was a twang too snug.

A few items correlated, culminating asudden in one of Tech's impressions, "So the time you worked at an inn and set clock radios to wake guests early in the morning with blaring rock music wasn't an accident."

Their phone discharged a succession of clicks.

The engineer materialized to scoop it up. "Why are you telling me this?" He cut the line forthwith. "We've been reorganized. Our two targets "are merging. Al Qa'ida is moving in."

"The Base and The Foundation? The Rule versus The Establishment?" Ayr systematizes. "No way," invoking her words be true.

"Step it up," selectively picking for his instruments on the quick.

"They're here, now?!" Comp-Sci's rucksack nimbly refilling.

"As of this instant we've intercepted messaging and their activity level has increased sharply."

"Preparations," paraphrases Tech.

"Soon, the real deal."

"I miss a proper burning effigy block party."

Tech amends, "Our southern cousins had them too."

"They're saving us a trip, anyway," Comp-Sci harping on the car ride.

"I can't appreciate what's more treacherous."

"Absolutely, and our information teams know every rock out here and will provide constant real-time communication. We form a perimeter, control movement around fixed group one, and group two scrambles straight into expectant us. Expectant us," the engineer reiterates for safety purposes.

"Remember their objective: success means we all die.

"Suicide is no obstacle, but a given. Count on them being wired, heavily armed, hurling explosives, and don't allow any getting close."

"What about the Arabs?"

"Ideas have a life of their own," fancies Maliya.

The shanty's accoutrements' rustic aura is sponged by Green Eyes, "If I take a nap, will there be a cat on me when I awake?"

"If there is," Aram allays, "probability says Ofer will eat it."

Meal three. "Then I'll be ready."

"So tell me, what was Mr. Roberts like before he went on a machete rampage and slew his family?" practices Ben as newscaster.

Aram bites, "He was a really nice guy."

"Quiet, kept to himself, took in strays, shovelled our walk," Ben doubling roles to expand his range.

"A good neighbour. Yeah, we really liked him. I can't say I noticed anything different."

"Did I mention he loved cats? Though none ever bothered us. Not...a...one."

She restarts, "Contemplating the abstract, consequently projecting that brainstorm into written "and spoken word. So it's in the air to be picked up."

"Maliya, am I to glean psychic bugging?"

Ben rags Aram, "You tell me."

"Actual communication is via wavelengths and transmitters. Should the sensorially imperceivable be otherwise?"

"Guessing the radio song before it's turned on," Aram illustrates.

"Whether or not we can audibly hear it, the broadcast wavelength is present. Sensitization to a well-used frequency would cause us to hearken the station during silence. Increased volume is only signal amplification, anyway, until we can aurally discern."

"Instinctively the listener hunts back to the source. We read people by familiarity with the chain of their actions. Patterns."

"The dog always knows before you do," Ben wraps.

"Not requiring electronic media to connect..."

"...thoughts mold the world."

"And here everyone is, harping on weapons of mass destruction."

"On the motif of people talking," Yuli insinuates, "is culture language-biased, with high-pitched tones cut off from the emotions as opposed to a low resonating grounded voice and personality?

"Also weigh relaxed smoothness of tongue versus a harsh staccato."

"Yes," conclusively in tandem.

Aram transcends, "An attitude: it's not 'working on it' as much as flipping a switch."

Maliya, concordant, "Change your mind. That's all."

"This is their game," commiserates Ben.

Yuli slumps.

The engineer doled out disparate individual routes of procession which ultimately should secure that the Canadians ring the Israeli cabin and choke it. "Tech, the direct course from here to just short of there," slicing his karate hand through a mountain.

"I didn't realize my distaste for rappelling until just this second."

"Tech, you've got the crow's nest," imparting its significance.

"I'll keep watch." He toted appropriate gear for a rock assignment and stomped ground.

"Comp-Sci, by the water. Through it if needed."

He and Ayr were fazed.

"The animal kingdom?"

"Become part of their natural environment and

"they'll signal when a stranger crosses the area." A pamphlet is bestowed, "Read this."

"'Do not confront any bear that could be at the site - Transfer Station Public Notice'. These are guidelines for the regional dump." Broaching the unknown, perusing the material, "'Do put all...small children out of your vehicle...into bins.'"

"And I'm on the circuitous path to the far end."

With an air of certainty, "Never happen."

"You trot with until we reach your side," producing horses in duplicate.

"Oh no."

He tackles his mount as it skitters and haphazardly bashes and bounds off its equine brother, "Simple, Ayr. I was once young and antisocial and my parents got it in their heads that I was a special needs child and signed me up for therapeutic horse riding. While the autistics and paraplegics got their pick, the school leftovers, needless to say, had a bit of an attitude. Mind the pun."

Ayrden skipped from bustling hooves as the second saddle acted quarrelsome.

The engineer wasted no time asserting dominance by crop and a summoning backward. It reared and kicked, barely submitting its gait aft. "Here "you go," he offered as the brute snorted, his eyes crazy aware, ears aerodynamically sleeked to racing mode.

"You expect me to get on that savage? At first he seemed harmlessly mischievous. Now he's angry."

"Right. Git." It tore toward a well-grassed paddock.

"My plan?"

"Line 11," holding up two parallel fingers and walking them like legs. "Follow me as much as you can. Don't be late."

Chapter Six

Remote is the coming light soft as candles. Members of the cottage shrouded in veils of deception. "You're not seeing the whole picture."

"Did you hear...?" Yuli misunderstands Aram's tour guiding.

"Night hawks choked."

"What?" she fills in space, still on first phrase.

"Bash of the waterfall. Which note is it?"

"Whither the coyote meets lightning," Ben cuts his koan tartly, "which reminds me, where is the rotter who flushed you continent to ocean, reprise, and why is his henchman sleeping? Ladies and gentlemen, while you stuff intellectualist egos with the metaphysical platitudes of your esoteric conversations..."

"Chary, you could hurt something," Aram remarks on Ben's sheer volume of syllables in such rare concentration.

"...the spooks are stalling. Impending catastrophe, I can poke it out of my spasmodic lungs it's so palpable. They're consuming time. We might have considered ourselves fortunate to hold on another moment, but it's the opposite. We have to abscond."

Indifferently, "You just got that?"

"What if," Ben launches on dry parody, "we could see life from the eyes of a Buddhist? How to show a layman what a meditator uncovers by simply viewing everything a different way? Merging hard science and philosophy, feasibly with some cool pictures. Wouldn't that be swell?"

Maliya swallows the premise, "The difficulty is in exposing the atomic world to a recording device without changing it."

"It would scare the daylight out of you, that's what it would do! Do you think it's easy being a saffron, caught between Hebrew 'principal' and Arabic 'whatnot' as his energy transforms Greek rhythms?"

"Since you've put it out there," by precursory depth Aram is moved to default mode with Maliya, "medical imaging techniques could measure the monk's changing state of awareness as he enters another plane."

"They don't pay enough attention to fields around the patient."

"Ancient eastern practice."

"Totally."

"Yeah dude," interlopes Ben, "and is it not apropos to bring to this confab thermally videotaping "digestion? Tonight's feature: calories and heat."

"Interfaces!" Maliya, whetted. "Photograph electrons of a finger meeting a table."

"Why aren't researchers interested in unlocking the mystery of God?" with renewed perturbation. "Why, why leave The Guy to humble experts on mountaintops?"

Flip Aram bites, "Because it isn't a particle running around a gigantic track really really fast?"

"I've been to makyo, darlings, and it ain't pretty. Just like Eyes over there, only they weren't attached to a body. Pairs and pairs of eyeballs, translucent, suspended in the room, not resembling human form, all staring at Ben. Even now, microscope transparencies give me the sweats."

"For me, Yuli, it's people who refer to themselves in third person."

"And the psychologists bone up on reality."

In truth, while individuals from the Israeli factions were slowly clueing in to their circumstance, the local ensemble hit a number of minor snags reaching point.

"What is your position?" The engineer did not receive response. "Relay your coordinates. Ayrden. Ayrden, call in."

Static over the wire.

"Blasted..."

"I was afraid this was going to happen," Comp-Sci calmly articulates prior to hotfooting it through the backwash, an infantry of miffed geese nipping and flapping in hot pursuit.

The engineer tabs the next one, "Comp-Sci, are you on target?"

Panting dispatched.

"Comp-Sci."

"Not...now! Huh. Huh. It's that nightmare all over again. Ah!"

"What...a...gale."

"Ayrden?"

"Gale! At one juncture I was sure I'd make more progress on my hands and knees."

"Are you advancing?"

Sound of wind like a train. "I was right."

Gusts then came way of the engineer, an outburst angling an overpowering knock toward the ground. His horse stumbled, and so, part way down, must have decided to recover by dumping him along with his top-heavy shoulder cargo. He had to wear the unbalancing paraphernalia for such an event in a bid to prevent its loss which, agreeably, facing the sky from this supine pose, suggested more than a hint of irony.

Tech overheard the ruckus on the com by virtue of nook on the bluff lee side but was unavailable for comment. Much as the climber currently stood at preferable assessment rating in comparison to his team, a singsong cricket had found perch on his pack and insisted on serenading him an irksome single-pitched tune the entire vertical trek. During those seconds of intense concentration, precisely when he went to grab a hair further out, the pest would reliably squeal through ears and brain and he'd slip off into the welcoming support ropes perpetually being rigged and reset.

"Hey everyone, Ofer's back," Ben toots. "We were curious about your conviction...on a matter."

"When you find her, you'll lose her," forecasts Grenade to Yuli and Aram who remain unbaited.

"Another verse. And you brought a gift. May I open, to see if it's good?" no intention of handling the object.

"I don't care. Snared it lying on the ground."

"Moon plots: worthwhile investment? Pro? Con?"

"Thought it was asleep, ready to stomp it. Didn't have to."

Chapter Seven

"Status," summons the engineer mid-tramp. "All reply."

"Breathing, last time I checked," clears Comp-Sci.

Ayrden trifles, "What part of 'I don't supply information over the phone' don't you understand?"

"This would be an appropriate time for an abduction," lastly, dangling. "How? I'm not fussy."

"Tech, have you done anything on the mission control situation?"

"What on earth are you talking about?"

"The master. Have you set up the toys?"

"Frankly, no."

"Well, do it."

"Get Tech to clamber up a butte. Get Tech to affix and calibrate ticklish technological gadgets to the peak. When did I become the crew's lackey?"

"Get Tech a cosy paycheque and public service benefits."

"And I'd like world peace...and dessert."

Comp-Sci interpolates, "You clambered up a butt?"

"They promised me aerospace engineer."

"Ayrden?"

"Ayrden?"

"That's what my creditors write in big red letters. So, I put in the application and this is what came out the other end."

"I brought you into this field," the engineer owns, "literally."

"No!" croaks Comp-Sci.

"Better than television," Tech grades.

"Thanks, en-gi-neer."

"Sorry. You possessed the necessary skills."
"Skills?"

"Ayrden?" the back-chatter prattles on.

She answers in good faith, "I for one relish a propitious five a.m. march."

"'Forced march' surpasses that."

"It was in..."

Collectively, "...the brochure!"

"Ayrden, tell them what else they've won."

"'You can look forward to cooking your own food, participating in sports activities, attaining a coveted appointment overseas.'"

"And over dale."

"Coveted by an Afghani sniper, presumably."

"Tech, what are you in for?" Comp-Sci sifts.

"I'm a filmmaker embracing no money, no clout, no audience."

"Ah, you're an independent filmmaker."

"Explains the scrawny." The engineer canvasses Comp-Sci, "What's your excuse?"

"Staying light on my feet, able to leap small doors from an open window."

"Tall buildings."

"Yours sounds much harder."

"Maybe there's the problem," emits Tech on his assemblage.

"Could be a lot of them."

"I'm afraid so," Comp-Sci negotiates.

"Closed the tower? Not to despair, somewhere there's bound to be another single," the engineer boosts.

"More or less."

"Women love a postman."

"Yuck!" Ayrden rebounds. "I just bagged that."

"But not too long, or you'll fall asleep. Tech, headway?"

"Well, basically it reacts to its own stimuli without any control on my part."

"Yea."

"No comment."

Her voice triggers Tech, "What are Israelis like, Ayr?"

"Besides the casual breaking into song?"

"Says it all."

Comp-Sci is not sated, "No, I require details on the tropical girls."

"Specifically? Cases, trunks of lame stories at the U.S. consulate for visas to follow their boyfriends studying abroad so they wouldn't lose them to anything along the lines of free will, world exploration, growing up."

"Ouch."

"Still eager to deliver your package?"

Tech, exploring, "And the other way round?"

"While vacations hotel-visit a stunning topography, permanent residency offers the extra pleasure of handling local customs and attitudes, complaints about what your dog did to whomever's lawn. They'd like you to reseed."

"My family's idea of touring a foreign country was stuffing everyone into a rented compact car and bickering down European highways. Mmm, the nighttime dive. We absorbed culture like mileage."

Grenade was cool, a man without worry, like it was over yet nothing was done. "Late Prime Minister of words, you didn't catch the game before you? All this time since you met her. Blind."

"Too early for the villain's confession. No?" Ben shores his side.

Aram doesn't speak. Something of Ofer's victory march rings true.

Yuli studies her brother-in-law's mien.

Again nudging, "It was serendipitous seeking refuge in the islands?"

"The Pacific name. We got that miles ago," the aide minimizes. "News flash: non-Israeli designations in Israel don't go unnoticed for long."

Aram continues in still watch.

Maliya is nervy.

Green Eyes wakes and happens to block himself at the entry.

"I put it right there, hiding in the open. The plan. The doubt. The inherent cross-purpose. Can't anyone count anymore?"

"Count!" leaks Ben. "Right," frantic for what.

Loud saying naught, Maliya draws all's scrutiny.

"Maliya," with his habitual pointing. "Ten, thirty, forty, and five. Eighty-five."

She corrects, "You forgot the ayin, another seventy."

"Aram forgot the eye, too, if I've been following our nemesis here, but he really followed me "here. That's not the point now. It can go either way."

"Fae," Yuli submits. "Eighty-one."

"Alephs and hehs are similar, vowelish. They've morphed over time so are not fixed entities in this respect. Fae is also an eighty-five hidden in alternate spelling. Fae, Maliya. Maliya, Fae."

His mock introductions abraded.

Yuli nails it, "Even the original Fae and whitewash..."

Seed.

"...equal Maliya proper. The liberties..."

"...are witness as far as eternity."

"What, Fae?"

"Nothing."

"Inconsequential information," Ben arbitrates. "Neat, but useless."

Aram is not so sure.

The commander waits.

Grenade's signal to Maliya had manifested.

Fae rages, "I'm not returning to fighting the war and I won't kill Aram!"

"You?" Ben and Yuli accost.

"Don't have to," Ofer foments. "That's why they invented Arabs."

"And religious Jews," appends the

commander.

"Extremist anything, really," rounds out Ben.

"You let them go."

They thought Yuli was coercing the supreme spook.

"I did."

Aram zeroes in on Maliya.

"Supposed to, don't worry. What? I was in the arts troupe."

"My specialist," delineates the commander.

"You tortured her!" Yuli strikes.

"Trained."

"To do Ofer's bidding."

"And stand up to him."

Fae petitions Aram, "If one was to die, don't you think he'd know?"

"I'm so accustomed to living self-aware I'm out of touch."

"Well, I am not."

Ben dissents, "The girl's two people!"

"Many more," Green Eyes elucidates.

"Why is everyone so unhappy? I served both," blazons Fae. "Aram was removed from public office and Israel," she itemizes to Ofer. Then, pivoting to Aram, "And you're not dead."

Chapter Eight

"Best case scenario, I'd say," Ben synopsizes. "Way to sit on the fence."

Yuli skims by her semblant investigator, "Some have a knack for it."

"There's still this whole transglobal stalking episode, though."

"Not satisfied with the lack of bodies?"

"Wait wait wait."

"That's all we've been doing."

Grenade's incidental remark replayed. "He's using terrorists."

"Excuse me?" Fae contests.

"The other terrorists." Casting to his Prime Minister, "They'll get the GSS off the hook for your precedent assassination when you're murdered this time for real."

"There's bound to be a handful of Islamic Fundamentalist zealots somewhere athirst on perpetrating a senseless act of violence and destruction, as long as it can fit the doctrine," corroborates Green Eyes. "They're good for it."

Ofer moralizes with him, "Pitifully sad when your first inclination upon waking up in the morning is endamaging for purposes of money and power."

"Which gives you free reign to go after Iran," Aram bluntly deducing. "And Muslims don't drink."

"Yet one drafts images of bottles imbruing the crime scene."

"No one else from the developed world will break from talk long enough to act. Don't forget, we're first in the line of fire. Oh, a tear will be shed when Israel has been demolished, but after the tissue has been tossed to the garbage they'll find we're just as expendable."

"Like Poland," the commander illustrates Grenade's rationale.

"Or a canary," substitutes Ben.

"One has to be careful when given a free ride. The cost may turn out beyond what was anticipated."

"Yeah? I'll have you know it's fairly irrefutable Aram probably has a strategy, too," Ben deposes.

"Please," indulges Grenade, "I wouldn't want to encumber your potent measure."

"I wish somebody would end the suspense and let me in on the big plan," the commander fawns.

"He presumes the Canadians are on us."

Laughter.

"Non issue."

Aram inwardly reacts.

Ben, genuinely, "Why wouldn't the Canadians be on top of this?"

"Hey Tech, how's where you are for an infinity pool?"

"Spectacular, until the retaining wall gives and we get poured over the mountainside."

"That's what you're into?" endures the engineer as he cuts his satellite connection. "Fantasy yards?"

"I take my caffeine in chocolate form," Ayrden deals in.

"What?" Comp-Sci retorts. "Cold water, AC. Canadians like to simulate winter all year round."

"Deep and dark, innermost filling cocoa."

Tech surveys the lot, "All I'm saying is, after this goes off they'd better not play jazz at my funeral or I'm reaching up and dragging 'em down with me."

"When it's my time, I want to exit fast and quiet. Remember that, no keeping me around stuffed with tubes like some kind of ornament."

"Boo!"

"Oh!" Ayr clutches her heart, looking fatally shocked. "Yes, that's exactly it! Oh."

Evocative of an obscene phone call, "What d' ya want me to do with you' bohhhdy?"

In Toronto a CSIS agent leaves confidential documents parked in the company car.

"Now, who's path is right?" Ofer and Green Eyes agitate.

"There is no right one, just the one we are on."

"So anything goes?"

"Not at all. The future is at present, and the right path is the one that resonates with you."

"Religious, or crazy?" mulls Ben. "Sometimes both."

Yuli surmises out of step, "You always land the unwanted jobs."

"Is it my choice to take the available lot or does greater design funnel us through?"

"Hotels aren't about finding a physical place, but establishing a permanency in a place of mind. And a mall isn't for provoking a specific choice, rather a select state of mind."

"Dreaming vacation shopping again?" Aram keeps up.

Then Fae begins to meander, "Hell is depicted similar to the centre of the earth, heaven in the clouds. Life in the middle at pains refining its energy to the end of escaping above, being sucked grave into the "core the alternative."

"Thirty of silver spells end, you know."

"Also loathe, fear, all is over. All of a goblet."

"It transforms into Passover."

Ben lightens Aram with another exegesis, "Spend the summer?"

"Tal and I came here for the pregnancy!"

"Here here?" All question, inspecting the hutch.

"Hereabouts."

Yuli educed Ofer's notice.

"We should go out sometime," aptly propositions Ben.

"Like a date? Or two people hanging, having fun?"

"Let's start off as two people..."

"I can do that."

"It's a stretch," articulate the cheap seats.

"...and see how it goes."

Chapter Nine

"We have the right to colour!" Yuli promulgated to the Hell's Gate air tram. Regional designations inspire such confidence. Grizzlies cross the Coquihalla, perhaps get stranded in Hope, but to reduce import and inflation the Israeli government back home intentionally broadcast television solely in shades of gray.

Tal had already thought of names. "Ran, sweetie. Come, come here, mommy's cutie. Would you like a popsicle? Fae, drop it! Drop the cat now! What did I tell you? That's how you speak? Where do you think you are from? Approach quickly. What are you doing? No, don't touch, don't touch the...!"

"In true Middle Eastern spirit. It's like the world belongs to her."

"It does." They outran semi-laden traffic in downpour and mist, abiding mid-journey with bundles of cars on rock slides being cleared. Hydroplaning at the embankment edge, clenching the wheel and remembering where was that road, blinded by oncoming trucks. "I figure I'll give a couple of different ones a try, I have a good feeling about a few of them, and see who wins. Run! Run!"

"There you are, you just needed to lower your

"standards. Don't think in terms of desirable mates. Walking DNA. I should have known you were the reproductive equivalent of a piece of cardboard and to obtain swimmers from Gadi you'd have to go in and take them yourself. You two and the combined brainpower, still your stuff's not smart enough to let go."

"I've got to change my image to hot sterile chick."

"...which is funny because you were scaring away guys for years by wanting babies. Oh, the list. Choose your line carefully. Intelligence? Creativity? Given. Looks, although perdurable only a turn. Stubborn personality. That could be useful."

Doctors threatened an obligation to preventatively treat for cancer instead of fertilizing Tal's eggs with the arranged donor sperm temporarily withheld and teetering on the threshold of an interprovincial legal glitch. Repaired fallopian tube Old Lefty sustained as white coats preached their case based on protecting society from her moral irresponsibility while number 6721 thawed. "Are you on something?" her specialist inquired.

"Well, actually, it's not related."

"Hormone therapy, Tal."

"Right. Western Canada persists on the

"subject of rec-re-a-tion-al drugs. You would suppose so, wouldn't you?...No."

"Here's a slightly higher prescription to jump-start the process." Daring her resistance, "You know you want it."

The hotel flood shut off its main, elevator malfunctioning. "Young lady," Yuli prelected, "have you been up all night making porn?"

"Buyer's remorse. We paid so much money to feel sick. Ignore me," Tal insisted, clutching her abdomen, cloaked in a large t-shirt on the bathroom tile. "Everything's under control."

"You look like an animal. Species wriggled out of the mire to go to university only to revert back to this."

"I have so many problems between my waist and thighs I could simply cut the whole section out."

"Then food would fall straight out of your throat. Yeah, this was one of your better ideas."

"Why use these disposable daily ovulation tests when all I have to do is watch the collection of intoxicated strays outside my door?"

"Between that dog who follows you up and down the corridor and your ample bosom I'd differ with the conclusion of these violet watermarks. You're a human dairy factory."

"They assigned the torture nurse last time, but I showed her. I bled all over her floor. Watch me die. So there!"

"Maybe you weren't meant to define yourself as a breeder."

"Don't ruin the plan."

"Actually, you're doing quite well."

"I'm barely conscious."

"Still, better than I predicted."

"Do I want to know? Oh, entertain me. How did you envision my condition, lest it become a self-fulfilling prophecy?"

"More out of it. More pain. Definitely a lot more blood."

"Definitely."

"And you wouldn't be able to vacate at all."

"Beautiful."

"I watch catatonic parents tediously tending their young and all that comes through of their idiot-savants' cooing at some duncical exhibit is 'How annoying.'"

"I'll keep it in mind. Don't be bitter. Those sweet darlings of God-given smile, adored with custom 'aww', soon enough will grow into the world and suffer."

"Well, if it's Jewish-looking and lacks a

"savagely wounding humour it's his."

"I love this alien. I won't stand to be away from it for one second."

"Just the kind of smothering stalker every child dreams of."

"My gynecologist wishes to date you."

"So, tell him already. Give away the trick ending."

"Yuli."

"I don't know. Paying to stare at me over the dinner table, nervously wondering if he'll get to where he gets to in his office while he's on the clock earning a government paycheque when you strip yourself down - Blah!"

"Yuli!"

"...without pretense or commitment. I would've presumed presently he gets the better deal."

"At least stop discussing items on medbroadcast.com."

"Inclined to keep the masses ignorant and complacent?"

"Hey! Hezi the paraplegic finally committed to his long-standing girlfriend."

"See?" referencing her earlier words like a concordance.

"When it came time to smash the cup the

"couple sort of gaped at each other an awkward moment before half their relations pulled out hammers."

"No curiosity they married. He'd have had to soup up the rig to back out."

Tal collared her buzzing phone. "It's a firm 'no' for tonight, because I'm especially beautiful tonight and I can't guarantee how I'll be tomorrow? Man, you ride with danger. The doctor wants to speak with you," lending her cell to Yuli.

"Right. Yes. Glad to hear you've still got your own teeth," finishing the call. "He says he'll take his chances. Let me explain this, Tal. You essentially have a hot rendezvous with a turkey baster. You don't have to work it."

During her procedure Tal quizzed the medical staff, "Perhaps you could employ the loudspeaker and corral some more folk in here? There's standing room in front."

"If to retrieve that time you stopped talking."

"Private party with the ultrasound, unless you're willing to negotiate its return." She had prepared for hospital stay by markering a major sign which she smartly unrolled and taped over her sheets:

sleeping, not dead

Her finger following the written message, "Regarding signs of life in a coma, I am not to be cut up into tiny organ-size pieces. No more Mexico for this one."

"Ten. Nine."

"You realize that if I'm buried at Thompson River Estates..."

"Five."

"...coyotes will dig me up."

"Patient's under."

Tal awoke groggy, "Was that you crooning La Traviata? Nice touch. Cultural...*misterioso...*"

"The obstetrician said he had never seen such a large head on a girl," Yuli recounts.

"She must have been really glad that happened," winces Ben.

Invested Fae disparages, "Doesn't he think he's the slickest item to ever pop out of a uterus?"

"Ofer's mama dressed him in dresses," retaliating.

"We were religious," sets the wrathy agent.

"Good plan. Look how that turned out."

Chapter Ten

> Réveille! (tee-tee-tee tah)
> Réveille! (tee-tee-tee tah)
> C'est les soldats qui viennent.
> (tee-tee-tee tah)

"Ayrden, we're exhausted and can't sleep and your plagiarized Acadian tune broadcasts are giving us nightmares."

"We're on point," the engineer fills in.

Comp-Sci kindles his lethargy with fresh topic, "How is that New France franchise working?"

"I'll have one Vignettes, two Riel and Friends, insert political enemy and hold the fries," Tech lightly roasts.

"I'm developing an interactive Colonize Canada DVD featuring all your favourite characters in unbridled fashion. Yes, you can even have Marguerite Bourgeoys actually setting the torch to Brulé's stake when:

    a) the Huron aren't looking
    b) the Iroquois are all off chasing Magdelaine de Verchères, or
    c) the Haida are busy sending thank-you

smoke signals to the Intendant upon
reception of smallpox-contaminated
blankets and their children's church/
boarding school education.

"Would you expand worldwide?"
Tech hatches, "Trainees!"

"Ah toi, berre hiwonderre qui vorre ici,"
rendering in off-colour non-period accent. "Hey,"
interested.

"And she teaches impressionable youngsters."

The engineer imparts that a scout might be
indispensable.

"I tell you, we lost Jimmy to the water bowl
last week!"

Ayr marches on the oblique with Tech, "Yes, I
can be of service without being a sacrifice. Please get
the subtle difference."

"Can't we just hand them to the Americans,
rid ourselves of the problem?"

Comp-Sci, a capella, contracting the
circumference alongside, "That's not bad, you know.
Partners in crime. Let them act, the big power. We
have to retain our image, which benefits us both."

"Leak it."

Pausing, attending his team's conclusion,

"Already been done."

After the engineer had made his proclamation all ears accused Ayrden of providing the intel.

"Why is everyone always suspicious of me?"

Continuing the briefing, "Only timing could snarl the scheme."

"Ayrden's acting strange again," Tech churns.

"Again?"

"Taking notes to an épaulette button microphone," pitching up a gradient.

"What's up with her?"

"Someone thinks she's in the secret service."

"Secret service blend in," she faults. "That's what they do. They don't stand out so as to forget them as soon as they're gone."

"Eh, you're not in the service unless they actually tell you you're in the service."

"Ah, but it's secret," Comp-Sci reminds Tech.

"And they turned off your shirt forty minutes ago when the sound guys went home."

"Hold on, hold on! The engineer didn't supply the how."

Thusly, he decrypts the puzzle, "Think Arab market."

"Fitting."

"By walking away you compel others to come

"after. A snub manifests superiority. It lures to the brink of tunnel vision."

"Much appreciated your slithering into the do-the-right-thing box," applauds Ayr.

Fleering, "Look which double mole is suddenly straight and pure."

"Fine, it's Captain. If it helps, you can picture me with a cape."

"That won't be necessary."

"All the same, the forgery snap was très cute," Tech dropping a binocular eye on a later Ayrden as she reflected on aging.

"I don't know that girl of perfect and naïve complexion."

"Still, you wouldn't switch places?"

Comp-Sci, comparatively confused, "With herself?"

"Squad, just a reminder..." the engineer underscores.

"No," she heels.

"...maximum speed is our minimum speed."

"Uh, I'm facing some...uh...Free-fall anyone?"

"Next victim," organizes the controller com.

"Covering twice as much ground as humanly possible. No need to concern yourselves. Not dif-fi-cult. I'd elaborate," wheeze, "if I could."

The pickets needle, "I always suspected you'd get places."

"When does the carrying portion of this walk begin?"

"It was amusing when you were in pain, but now not looking so great from this perspective."

"So, how is everyone today?"

"Command is supposed to be warm and nurturing."

He snickers.

"Seriously, what about the support to our fragile psychological state?"

"Yeah, where is the love?"

They burst.

The engineer transitions posture, "Good morning, Ralph."

"Good morning, Sam," Tech comes about.

"Ayrden."

"Guilty."

"We've hit the hot spot."

"Picked a hell of a place," adverts Comp-Sci.

"Where all secret service are history grads and bikers in Porches were firemen."

"You got it. That's the one."

"Just checking in to see you've not gone cabin fever."

"Or loosened any lug nuts."

"Well, we're a bit late then, aren't we?"

From her scope, Ayrden has a hampered visual inside the property, "What's happening?" relying heavily on audio. "Do I have to do something? Is it really urgent? Are there horses involved?"

"I wonder when it'll click that the Arabs aren't coming?"

Yuli stood fast to the cliff's edge and captured the vast blue sea accepting its river's flow with the dead at her arm. Here she had arrived. Knew the how, not the why. Where to after was not hers to foresee, along for the ride. Yet this moment would not remain and neither the place. One cannot force movement immobile to comfort and annihilate the spirit.

Unstable Ofer could have been swapped for a heavy oily jar of poison and it would have made no difference. "Don't be myopic. Nitroglycerin stops the sickness," reading as he'd been cast.

"Ah, but that depends on how you calibrate your instrument," marks Aram. "Stare until all is blurry, focus to be out of focus, and a supplementary visual field emerges which may reveal truths beyond what we already suppose."

Ben, overreached, "What does that mean?"

"The ability to project ourselves onto a sphere just outside the body which we then see as our environment though it's all us."

"Aren't those two disparate methods of meditation?" Fae parts.

"That's a sound question."

"Would music help?"

Irrepressible darkness. Again she flies. A journey is yours if you put it in your mind. Right, then I'll fall and we'll meet in another ten years.

Grenade hovers over the psychologist who slept not at rest, "You hold much in your head, stories revealing mysteries of legend from humble origin through headlines, divine purpose passing the enemy notoriety. Tell me, do you easily nightmare?"

On each arm a male and female guide floating pointed toe inches upon the earth, light enough to cross the bridge back in time. It eludes Yuli in a group of friends being chased as their escape vehicle slows at the critical point where dream travellers move faster than bullet on its trajectory.

"Order of magnitude," Fae liberates. "When extra sensory perception and communication alter electronics we then have an indication of which level of wavelength energy is involved in the former by studying the mechanics of the machine."

"Is this just for practice or will there be a test?"

Yuli awakens to Ben's query.

"Must consume all while there are still bugs that crawl," he continues, recommending a recess to Green Eyes. Then the aide noticed Grenade intense. "The intifada back home has been a disaster since Sharon hit the Temple Mount," suggesting that Aram was no longer relevant, "and it all happened without you."

Grenade smiled back half-mouthed.

The commander switches to Ofer, "I thought only we did that."

Glare traversing from his comrade to Ben, "Did you really think Israel would just give away everything?"

"And I thought the government ran the country," Aram exhales.

"Shouldn't you be off in the dunes disturbing the peace? Time is somebody somewhere enjoying tranquility. We can't have that."

Green Eyes took the bait.

Ben didn't sway Grenade.

"Ofer, the bottom line is you don't presently have the authority for my execution. The GSS had you marginalized as a rogue element. That plot is "defunct."

"Haven't you heard of swarm collective intelligence by individual actions?" he rebuts bluntly.

"Watch, you're a spook in a foreign country. Operations are illegal abroad, more so among friendlies."

"Illegal is illegal. No sense in turning up the heat on a boiling pot," Ben, a step behind. "More so?"

"We entered customs using fakes," itemizing. "The whole province length is lined by water so we could've run the border, and it hasn't occurred 'Why Canada?'"

Fae's commander concentrated on her words.

"I ask why every hour on the hour," the gritty engineer comments to Ayrden's translation.

An eavesdropper, vivaciously, "I know, I know."

"Shhh."

"The late Prime Minister can't return from the dead," Ofer promises last.

It clicked. "Probably about now."

Chapter Eleven

"They expect us to deliver him from the assassin," the Canadians decrypt.

"Swell."

Ayr senses being cornered, "Played a bit close to the chest, no?"

"Good we caught it."

Offended, "In the end you'll lose a recruit but gain..."

"Tell them what they'll gain, Johnny!"

"...a defamation of character legal action."

"Oh, I don't know. A girl could walk her dog one night, get hit over the head by some thug, and never return home."

"How randomly descriptive."

"When you care enough to be killed by the very best."

"Ahh, just don't presume you're working to your own end," she cautions.

"Not done yet," they are posted.

"So what's our policy on ally spies committing murder on their own head of state who has already officially died?"

The commanding officer alerts, "Mind their positions."

"Oh this isn't good."
"Heads up!"

Within the cabin belly tempo motioned slow. Premonitions of seers set to transpire. "This is where our paths diverge." Grenade drew a pistol from beneath his sticks-casual flannel duds keenly disguising a light floral island tourist getup and directed aim toward the party leader as he had many months before.

But Fae was in the vicinity of Ofer's blast. She ought not to have been in the manner that Aram had devised her arrest. He, too, harboured intentions when announcing their arrival in such a way at the forty-ninth parallel. Companion Maliya would have been rent from his arms and into jail, and safe from pursuers. He calculated wrong. A simple illicit paper, bogus name, would not have sufficed to bring out the cavalry. Fae knew. In her process she gambled the nature of her pseudonym, what it represented. Was the genuine citizen she portrayed in a placement somehow conflicting with her admittance? One of the dearly departed intelligence inclined to reanimate? Or perhaps she was the girl of which were heard rumblings of being under suspicion watch while in Israel? A traveller of interest to Fae's associates may range from public nuisance through potential terrorist to alien government employee, the latter holding true implying a high security clearance overseas ergo close tracking of all movements by said source. Ayrden didn't come across a terrorist. Fae banked on her not being a mere nuisance.

Ben leapt to intercept the discharge. He got a rush from posing the hero though the fretting quite dampened nerve sensation to his legs. On this pass he made it to the limo and that was his sole objective as he pained to just get in the way. He would not succeed.

Green Eyes spied a red dot place itself on Grenade's face.

The engineer managed to align the laser guide of his high-powered sniper rifle through one of two hut windows straight onto the gunman, conceivably blowing an uninterrupted hole out the back wall and onto a member of his team. "Ayrden's in the line of fire. Has someone else got the shot?"

"No."

"No," Tech calls, "You're it."

"Ayrden. Ayrden, adjust your location. Respond!"

She heard, but she was also entrenched in an

awkward bowl of a locus which, albeit regrettably, perfectly complimented the remainder of the unit for most other functions save this particular sharpshooting.

"Undershoot. Dull it. Dull the carry-over."

"Recalibrate and defocus," Comp-Sci seconds, the weapon's innate resistance to such a function notwithstanding.

As shots were fired Yuli had been grabbing to restrain Fae from a deadly plunge between darting bullets, Ofer and Aram. Aram was hit.

Green Eyes plowed through his charge, aunt yet doggedly clamping onto Fae's smatches of hair and fanning hems, and shovelled them both onto the floor while he made for his superior. He knocked Ofer off line, but losing him as buffer posed formidable continuity ramifications for Ayrden.

The Canadians invaded. "Let's clean out their sinuses," comes the order.

Loading a canister, "You're familiar with tear gas." It shattered the window from where the earlier bullet had left a clean hole and danced a hopping burning-smoke spiral in the structure interior.

"We won't be going in with rubber duds."

"Or water hoses."

"No subtext of malevolence here," due to the events surrounding what turned out to be Ayrden's last shift.

"And if there was, you don't possess technology capable of detecting it." They apprehended the Israeli transgressors without contest. Some even less than that.

Gas seeped outdoors over the bound and bleeding as they were hauled and lined up crouching down in the sand. Tech, Comp-Sci, and the engineer colluded anent what to do with them. Keenly assessing: Armed provocation. Sensitive subject matter, personages. Relatively insular crew activity. Onlookers none.

Chapter Twelve

The Canadian team dematerialized from that region to eschew possible repercussions from any rival factions, not the least of which since the tainted Arabs had vanished in the hands of the Americans. As those were delivered in secret and scattered broadly about Middle Eastern governments of antiterrorist stance on the basis of suspicious activity, jailed indefinitely without charge, tortured, the Canadians were reincarnated in fresh terrain themselves. Tech planted her urn under one arm, settled deep in the overgrowth of his partner's property, and eulogized. "Ayr would've loved the dry desert air in the summer, until a predatory bird swooped down and scooped her up."

"She prided herself on being one hundred percent here. If not, a part of her was," evaluates Comp-Sci, "there."

"You went out in good form," the engineer commends the container. "Very trim."

"Same to you," Tech ventriloquizes with raspy voice.

"And you," directed toward Comp-Sci.

"Why, thanks. I was just noticing my upgraded sensible meal and workout schedule starting "to pay off."

The engineer questioning the source of a Santa Claus and reindeer scene painted around the jar, "What is that?"

As Tech reaches inside, picking a flavour, "Cookies," the removal of its lid prompting jubilant Christmas marching music to chime. "Oh, and I brought the band."

"Ayr would have hated this," mocking her funeral.

Their officer biting in, "Just as well she's dead then."

Comp-Sci joined the eating. "Ah, well, at least we get the day off."

The wake lapses in the course of torsos launching into rotations, heads crooked, one's hand aimlessly glazing his own scruff of neck and they appraise the rustic acre, "A human being actually lived on this site?"

"That remains to be seen."

"Becoming," the engineer and Tech parley.

"Real! But she could've weeded the lawn. I lost Comp-Sci yon last hour."

"I don't know. It appears to be fall rye."

"What's that?"

"Grass."

"Grass? Looks like wheat."

"It's just like grass."

"Oh yeah, it's grass," unconvinced. "Six foot tall grass with a seed tuft at the end."

"Did you see how much space they left between segments of the doublewide?" Comp-Sci flags. "Burglars won't break in as much as sidle-shimmy through the centre."

"I heard every time she took a bath the house flooded."

"So she manifested a gargantuan hole in her floor?"

"Congratulations on your purchase, ashes and all."

All raising a beer, "Here here!"

"What's with the sprinkler on narcotics?"

"No returns!" blares Comp-Sci in a flurry, "I hold shares in Canadian Tire."

"Now that's sad."

Tech, fidgeting with the settings, "Maybe it waters better when not whipping 'round at fifty miles an hour."

"Hey! How 're ya doin'?" the engineer nonchalantly asks past the others.

"I'm not falling for that," Comp-Sci contests shakily.

Tech, apprehensive, is intrigued.

"What? Do you think I'm seven again and this is the first time you ask me if I want to go fly a kite and you act like it's going to be really fun but we just freeze a pose, arms standing in the air, cramped, complimenting the heavens?"

"Ooh, baggage."

The engineer paraphrases, "One knows he hasn't established a good rapport when he greets nobody walking into the room and a real guest turns around assuming the host is talking to someone else."

"What room? I wish. We're in a...field! If only there existed a room not hung with laundry."

"Or kleptoed from work. I noticed it's all regulation."

"No wonder she didn't quit. How would she have furnished her home?"

"You mean the rodent halfway house?"

"Ah! That's who you were addressing," Tech recomposes the engineer's gambit.

"By the way, those field mice forwarded a list of complaints as to the accommodations: Thumbs up for the oversize pellet and water bowls but last night taking a dip an entire generation almost drowned, the yummy peanut butter blobs on little tiny metal trays haven't been replenished in days, and that cozy "vacuum-snout hairy beast molting nest insulation has got to go."

Then the military purpose of their expedition crept in. "It's time we perform a sweep of the premise."

"I agree. The place could use a cleanup."

"Not me," Tech stretches, "That's why a career man takes a wife."

"God knows Ayrden should've."

"Curiously a feat which you nevertheless until now have not been able to defeat," the engineer shouldering him to their gadgets.

"But not in the gay way," Comp-Sci tails. "Then again, it's been a while, so who knows?"

The inspection bends the engineer and Tech on a return course, "Jim. Dan. Fredo. What's her mutt's name?" as Ralph dogs the lead.

"And what language does it speak?"

Comp-Sci tagged after the three.

Yet taking readings, they all veered again in formation.

"I'll never make it," Comp-Sci, hunched, knuckles drooping as an orangutan's, forward and back.

"It's only the second lap."

Eyeballing a meter the engineer pinpoints

besides, "The end is right there."

"If you hadn't performed those hyperactive circles of us at the outset you could've established a workable pace," Tech throws behind.

"A moment...Done."

"Hey Terminal, got any energy for some no-handed spotted push-ups?"

"Sure, Tech," revivified, "How many are you good for?"

"Guys, does this pet need a haircut?"

"Shipping out?"

"By the fur tracks we can infer there's a cheap clipper close by."

"If Ayrden's coiffure was any indication."

The engineer draws a snap from his jacket, lately pocketed from Ayr's effects, "Did you catch the mug shot?"

It circulates. "I never knew Ralph was famous!"

"Why?"

"So Ayrden could show she met him."

"But it's not a picture of Ayrden, it's the dog and..."

"Ralph kissed me once," Comp-Sci, bragging sheepishly.

"As long as he doesn't write 'occupation:

"'soldier' on his customs form."

"Student. Student," the technician indents into memory. "You always pen 'student'."

"Relax."

"Now, there's an idea."

"Yeah, let's chill."

"Right."

Two of the bunch stare skyward in sync uninterrupted among tosses of ale and crunching chips.

"And it cannot be stressed enough," Comp-Sci's nose in a manual, "no matter how tempting, you are not to look in the direction of, even if you are under the impression that you cannot see..."

"...an end to these inane," Tech peeks to quote the subject listed on the handbook, "automotive instructions?"

"A pinhole camera must be used to indirectly watch the sun during an eclipse."

"Absolutely."

"Here here!"

Ralph flew at Tech's potato crisp and triumphantly chomped it from his easy fingers.

"When I die I'm gonna work for the Mossad."

Chapter Thirteen

Following the shootout the Canadians had set
to lay out a course intended for the smooth departure
of their secured Israeli guests. For her part, Yuli was
merely a tourist. Opting to run out the rest of her visa
in a cross-country drive over the Rockies, through the
wind-tired plains, to the maritimes, she established
that the cliff views of B.C. and undulations around the
lakes of Ontario were a stimulation amply
compensating for the price of being free. Finally alone,
it occurred to her that she truly wasn't. The world
held rhythm. God wields tools. They are the ways.
They are the stumbling blocks. Her loved ones yet
existed in the surrounds, in dimensions apart from
known reality not as distant as we fear. Flick a
switch. She had paid attention. Before the universe
came into being it was a dimensionless point infinitely
small. A meditation, a concentrated release, may yet
phase us to a mode without time and back to that
state where we are to the ends of the cosmos. Yuli
drove, knowing the topic of conversation on her
muted radio.

As an official of a foreign government Ben had
diplomatic status. He was discharged in order to
resume his duties, the duties of an aide to no one in a

fevered country swimming on a tether. Breaking loose being logical method to escape from the kicks of those flutterers headed in the other direction, naturally, they hook on tighter. Aram had revived in Ben during their brief contact in the bush the need for brave choices of progress, their necessarily involved risks, though he did not wish the second part particularly visit him and so settled to wield his negotiation skills in conflict resolution from the innards to avoid any swinging tips.

"You will be travelling abroad soon, MR Mara?" the engineer insinuates to his backward-reading interviewee.

"Absolutely."

"Excellent. There are incredible sights all over this time of year, unto the planet's corners for the avid trekker."

"Shortly I'll be so far off the beaten path it'll be like I was never here."

"Forgotten who you were already."

"Mislaid my name," amending.

"Right." Legally, this man without a country could have claimed status of asylum-seeker, but with the Canadians' precarious presence in a Middle Eastern war and a large Arab contingent living within its borders a deposed rosh memshala just bore mayhem as the last few days had perspicuously shown. The engineer handed back his papers.

On a personal level he and Fae had evolved into separate entities as a period apart from Israel they had marked, yet conversely the bond between them strengthened in a way that no expanse could diminish. So love gave room, still very much there. A meeting of the minds. Spiritual. How true. He wondered how much investment would be required to develop that soul camera. Maybe then he'd be able to distinguish who Fae was on a daily basis.

Chapter Fourteen

The third trumpet once again hit an incredibly discordant tone while diligently drilling a piece from repertoire. He stopped, then took a fresh whack at it from the beginning of that theme, repeating the same mistake. Undaunted, the player attempted further try. And another.

"Did you think if played enough times the note would mysteriously change in pitch?" chastises their conductor, wrapping him up with taps of baton. "Violins. Third movement, first notes of each arpeggio only. Now, doesn't that sing like a secondary melody to you? Please play it that way, thank-you. And from that leader sub-tune allow the remainder of each descending pattern to effortlessly fall downward as flowing water. A bow lift for every grouping will assist in painting this sound imagery as well as properly structure the technical aspects of your phrasing."

"But these pitches are unadorned," the concertmaster counts in. "Where does the composer make these markings? You're just creating method to increase the rigor," which happened to contradict his own instructions during sectionals.

"Yes. Also, the music screams out to be

"expressed in this manner. It's implied. Instinct."

At least the first string's inevitable overnight shift erasing and repenciling everyone's manuscripts would tickle the percussion.

"While we're on melodies and phrasing," eyebrowing, "winds. Brass isn't in the clear either. I guess that covers everyone who performs in a key. A musical sentence, similar to a spoken sentence, is one where we do not pro-nounce ev-ery syl-la-ble ro-bot-ic-al-ly the same." Dramatically, "Some words are more important than others. In like analogy, and interestingly conversely, we never open and close a sentence with rude jarring ACCENTS! Present company excluded," for the arts orchestra was a multinational consort. "Practice instructions."

"Maestro, are we doing all the repeats?"

"None."

Bows and sticks beat the stands with metric regularity.

"However, we're taking all the variations."

The hammering tapered off to reveal one trombone bluntly release a glissando and empty his spit valve.

"Alright, in a compromise you may perform half the variations at the beginning and the other half at the end. Our tactic is to learn, leave, and relearn the "material before production. Learn by repeating bars four times each, three times, twice, and once. Solid chords become arpeggios, arpeggios solid. Gain speed by alternating motifs fast then slow, slow then fast. For another exercise each bar is to be played three times perfect in a row before another bar is added, starting both from the time signature and finale."

"Union breaks in fifteen," the first violin whispers leaning in.

"Just enough," page placement reverts back. Arms raised, "Let's run movement one through on four."

As they launched the symphony trumpets stood to play their fanfare. In turn first trumpets rose and fell, seconds, then Ofer on third. By contrast, Green Eyes on trombone was rapidly sliding into the deliberate mischievous air of the piece.

"Crescendo."

Drums of every sort, palming, mallets, wove their way in. Through the density of merging voice, tuned and timbre, they threaded.

"No. No. No," whirling the bulk of the ensemble out of sync. His surrender, face rent with horror, "Rhythm correction. Triplets read as 'this is not dif-fi-cult dif-fi-cult this is not'. Re-cite this every night and you will play it right. As for the "timpani," breath, "I can't tell you you're wrong because you're supposed to concuss the house. Just not here," pointing at a hard rest in the latest bars opened on his podium score.

Ofer and Green Eyes hurled incriminating mugs as would angry pitchfork-wielding villagers have lobbed their torches stage left at Maliya and the likes in percussion.

Abruptly, "Again!"

The band smouldered on cue replete with its spies. Oddly, impersonating tie and tail performers was the next logical step after issue of a deportation order and the secret service were right into the rhythm of the thing. The key was in the symphony. Maliya, unsoundly, set her eyes upon Ayrden at her side. "How was Québec?"

"I was in Kingston."

"Ah, I guess it was no great shakes then."

"Probably not."

"How's your dog?"

"So outgoing, creating such an instant rapport with strangers, he makes me a better person."

"I'll take one for the weekend. There are some questions I need to ask his spirit."

"That's only a day. What?"

"They visit dreams." A nod as Maliya turns

the page, "Better make it two." Imminently touring Israel, the philharmonic was an aptly opportune benign cultural intermediary by which to administer a spy exchange between the two countries, the operation even coined in the temper of passport capriciousness.

"You know, a musical meditation such as this doubly serves to diffuse tensions within the trade, but of that subcontext apparently no one has informed your friends over there. Smile."

"Smiling. How long is this gig?"

"Paid for the season, total beach country blowout. I'll provide an electric xylophone pedal refresher. Up-down. Up-down."

"Bahgain basement piano wessons."

"Leahning so intense they won't heah you scweam," gumming in tandem, "Aaah!"

"When I Die..." was brought to cadence.

"Yah!" members whoop after the modern work's closing drum clap.

Ofer popped up next to the driver's seat to probe whether or not the conductor had any idea of the nature of his instrumentalists' substitutions. "That title, the one for Morrison's Symphony #1."

"'When I Die...'" Handily solved.

Restriking, "Aren't you afraid?"

"Of?" without turning his head from the mass of paper.

"'...the Mossad.'"

"The what?" ever so slightly clicking on a microbutton in his wand's handle while dispensing a theatrically dismissive wave.

"Last night I dreamt of opening a Hebrew dictionary with inlaid passages of wisdom from God in English from right to left," the girls get a leg up on Ralph, "And biblical pictures."

"Dictionaries define the meaning of words, the bible the meaning of life. So, what did he say?"

"'Time. Space. You don't need groups larger than eight.'"

"Germane."

"But what's eight?"

"Infinity. The transmutation of life cycles. Double mystical four. An octave. Shall I go on? Oxygen, that's always good. The tree of God is on the dictionary's eighth page."

"If you unravel the symbol it becomes nothing."

"Mastering professional cycling, they say, requires a leader and eight teammates willing to die for him. Although, behind the eight ball is a highly disadvantaged position."

"One piece that obstructs the game."

"If you had antlers you'd be royal."

"The small sail superior to topgallant is a mountain fanning down doling on each of a vast number an equal quantity. Therefore by means of the father...Father Father...door of door...pride of pride on high...I will destroy and be afflicted, be lost and perish ...he tied a bandage...he bundled a reed...a baby's sustenance...to unite...to love by way of he loved."

"Time. Space. God: the infinite, infinitesimal."

"The meekest instrument set in vibration by a breath." I can consume bread, partake of life's divine. I can engage in battle...I can devour war.